W9-BZP-033

Bird in the Hand

Ken Munro

Gaslight Publishers

Copyright ©1995 by Ken Munro
All rights reserved.

No part of this book may be reproduced or transmitted in any form or by any means, electronic or mechanical, including photocopy, recording or any information storage or retrieval system, without the express written permission of the publisher, except where permitted by law.

This book is a work of fiction. All characters and events portrayed in this book are fictional. Any resemblance to actual people or events is purely coincidental

Gaslight Publishers
P.O. Box 258
Bird-In-Hand, PA 17505

ISBN 1-57087-125-6

Library of Congress Catalog 95-67104

Printed by Professional Press
Chapel Hill, NC 27515-4371

Manufactured in the United States of America

98 97 96 95 10 9 8 7 6 5 4 3 2 1

Dedication

This book is for
Damian Tyler, my first grandchild.

Special thanks to
Capt. Donald Palmer, Jr. and
Lt. Tom Arnold, Asst. Fire Marshal

Chapter One

His parents had left him — for five whole days. But he didn't mind, too much. Not when a boy could spend those five days with his special friend, Sammy Wilson. A sleeping bag, a couple of shirts, some changes of underwear, socks, a toothbrush, and of course Sammy, would guarantee the stay-over to be an adventure. The two boys were Bird-In-Hand's budding detectives, and adventures always seemed to find them. What Brian did not know was that within the next five days, he and Sammy would be tied up by a bird, and he would be held hostage by a murderer.

Brian Helm shifted the load he was carrying as he approached the old wooden porch of the Bird-In-Hand Country Store in Bird-In-Hand, Pennsylvania. After carefully maneuvering several steps, he looked up at the "quilt of the day" that hung over a wooden bar that stretched between two pillars.

Today, the Amish-made quilt contained the Double Wedding Ring design. Each day the Wilsons displayed a different Amish quilt pattern and samples of the Amish-made crafts sold in their store. This display helped to motivate the millions of tourists who visited Lancaster County's Amish Country every year to spend, spend, spend.

The Bird-In-Hand Country Store was also home to Sammy Wilson and his parents. They lived on the second floor above the shop, Sammy's bedroom being to the right at the top of the stairs. Amish quilts, wall hangings, and other crafts filled the four small rooms of the shop itself. One exception was Sammy's area, a small glass display case that contained baseball and other sports cards.

He sat behind the case today as a large sleeping bag with arms and legs burst through the front door. Brian's face popped out from behind. "Hi, Sammy. I can only stay five months."

Sammy smiled. "I don't know if I can survive the five days. Let's see, today is Monday. Five days will make it through Friday. Okay, Saturday morning may I kick you out?"

"Yep," Brian grinned back. "My parents will return Saturday afternoon."

Sammy scooted out from behind the counter and grabbed the olive-green sleeping bag and led the way up the stairs to his bedroom. Brian followed, still clinging to his blue gym bag and his expectation of another fantastic adventure with his best friend.

Sammy's bedroom was more like a den. A wall-to-wall bookshelf filled with books and a large, old oak desk, supporting an elaborate computer system, dominated the room. The front wall contained one large window that overlooked Main Street. Weather charts, world maps, sport pictures, and various awards covered the end walls. A newly added bulletin board contained newspaper articles detailing two cases the two boys had recently solved, *The Case of the Quilted Message* and *The Case of the Amish Buggy Heist.*

The young amateur detectives, both fifteen, had been best friends since kindergarten. Strangely, the friendship seemed to endure *because* they were almost exact opposites. Sammy was tall and slim with straight dark hair and serious blue eyes. He was a super problem and puzzle solver and had many awards to prove it.

Brian, on the other hand, was short, had brown wavy hair, and devilish hazel eyes. While Sammy won awards for his problem solving, Brian won friends with his easy-going manner and humor. As long as he could remember, he had wanted to be just like Sammy Wilson. What he did not know was his best friend wanted to be more like him.

"Have your parents left already?" asked Sammy as he unrolled the sleeping bag on the floor beside the desk.

"Yep, my mother and father went on business trips to New York. My dad's doing his lawyer business stuff. Mom's checking on new computer hardware for her consulting firm. She also wants to spend some time at a health spa to lose weight. This is the first time they've gone together. I guess they needed a vacation away from us kids. Right, Sammy?"

Sammy enjoyed his partner's company. Brian's humor helped to soften his serious side and balanced his structured personality. He liked to bounce ideas off Brian, because Brian's off-the-wall questions stimulated his thinking. Having Brian as a friend was a way to escape from his impersonal and rigid, logical thinking. This was not their first sleep-over, but it was the longest so far and was certainly to be the most interesting.

Sammy slid open an empty bureau drawer. "Put your clothes in here." Then he added, "Where are your brother and sister staying?"

"With our Aunt Catherine in Lancaster," said Brian, throwing his shirts, underwear, and socks into the drawer.

Sammy shook his head. The drawer was now an island of chaos surrounded by an otherwise very orderly bedroom. "I suppose, you're going to throw your toothbrush into the sink, too."

The exaggerated movements of Brian's hands, playfully realigning his clothing in the drawer, told Sammy he was going to receive a typical Brian Helm response.

"If I had known you were going to be like my mother, I wouldn't have come," Brian said in mock irritation. He then stood at attention, holding his toothbrush out in front of him. "Now, sir, if you'll show me the appropriate resting place for my toothbrush, I will attempt to install it there to your satisfaction, sir."

Sammy laughed, placing his hands on Brian's shoulders. "Brian, please, please, please, don't ever change. Promise me you'll never change."

"Okay, I promise. Now will you unhand me? I must go and throw my toothbrush into the sink."

Five minutes later the two boys walked down the narrow stairway into the shop. Mrs. Wilson was in the quilt room straightening some of the many Amish-made quilts displayed on a bed and on movable metal arms that were anchored to the wall. A couple from Vermont were asking questions and looking for the one quilt that would be just right for their bedroom. Mr. Wilson was at the cash register shaking his head at something a large man was holding in front of his face. "Sammy, Brian, do you recognize the man in this picture? This gentleman wants to know if he might have been in the shop this morning."

Sammy glanced at the wrinkled photo of a thin, middle-aged man and then at the large, tough-looking stranger who didn't look at all like a gentleman. Probably a cop, thought Sammy, but not from around here. "No, I've never seen him."

"Well, if you see this man, give me a call at this number." He wrote a phone number on a piece of paper and handed it to Mr. Wilson.

"May I ask why you're looking for him?" asked Sammy.

The man frowned. "That's none of your . . . Look, it's a private matter. Just call me if you see him."

"And your name?" asked Mr. Wilson.

Glancing around the shop and noting that he was the center of attention, he replied, "Chet, Chet Kelley. Let's just say the man in the photo is my brother." He headed for the door and left the shop.

Mr. Wilson wrote the name, Chet Kelley, on the paper above the phone number. "What do you think, Sammy? Do they look like brothers to you?"

"No. Not even close." He walked over to the phone. "What's the phone number, Dad?"

After a few seconds, Sammy hung up, looking very confused. "What do you know? The number is the Farmland Motel."

"A man is looking for his brother and staying at the Farmland Motel. What's wrong with that?" asked Brian.

"Well, sometimes things aren't what they seem." Sammy reached under the counter and grabbed his camera. "Dad, if you don't mind, Brian and I are going out for a while."

Mr. Wilson smiled. "Going to take some pictures of the bad guys are you? Fine, just be careful."

"Come on," said Sammy as he poked Brian and headed out the door, across the porch, and into the warm August morning sun.

Brian threaded through a couple of tourists and ran to catch up with Sammy. "Hey, where're we going?"

"We have a new mystery to solve," said Sammy.

Brian looked puzzled. "Really? Great! But the man went the other way."

"No, no, forget that man. Do you remember last week when David Lapp's barn burned down? Gil Green said he wanted to make it a community project to raise money to help the Amish rebuild the barn."

"Yeah, it was in the newspapers. Oh, so the mystery is, who started the fire? Right, Sammy?"

"No, actually, the mystery is, who is The Bird?"

Brian's eyes narrowed. "I don't get it."

"You will. Look!"

Sammy pointed up the street to the Bird-In-Hand Farmer's Market parking lot. A crowd had gathered around a wooden platform supporting something covered by a large, blue drape. The material extended down over the front of the platform. Gil Green, thirty-eight, of medium height and build, was standing on the platform next to the cloth-covered object which was slightly smaller than Gil himself.

As the boys approached the crowd, they heard Gil Green say, "Some of you may not know this because you are visitors to our little village of Bird-In-Hand, but last week we had a fire. This fire destroyed an Amish barn, David Lapp's barn. The police now suspect arson. What we are trying to do here today, Monday, and the next four days, is to raise money to help the Amish raise a new barn. So we're asking you for donations to this worthy cause. And to make it interesting . . ." Gil Green pointed to his right.

Someone pulled at the blue cloth which immediately fell to the ground, revealing a person entirely concealed in a colorful bird costume. A large, painted human hand on flat plywood extended along the front of the platform which acted as the stage.

"So, folks, here we have it . . . a 'bird-in-hand!'" Gil Green paused.

Laughter erupted and the applause grew louder as the audience made the connection between what they saw and the name of the village, Bird-In-Hand.

Sammy wasn't sure if there was any truth to the old legend. The name Bird-In-Hand was supposedly created when two road surveyors, working on the Old Philadelphia Pike, also known as Route 340, needed a room for the night. When deciding whether to stay at the local inn or travel to Lancaster, one of them quipped, "Well, a bird in the hand is worth two in the bush. There's a place to stay right here. Let's take advantage of it." So they stayed at the local village inn which later became known as the Bird-In-Hand Inn.

"I'll be right back," said Sammy, and he ran to the front of the platform. Raising his camera to his face, he composed the picture and captured what he hoped would be a piece of Bird-In-Hand's history.

The Bird in the Hand had been one of Gil Green's ideas. New to the area, he had quickly made friends and became known as an up-and-coming businessman. His most recent business venture was developing a tourist attraction for children. It was to be called, Amish Virtual Reality. With the aid of advanced computer technology and electronic headgear, the children would be able to visit an Amish farm, play with the animals, climb a silo, and even experience a jump into a hay pile. All these activities would be accomplished while the children stood safely in a room on Main Street. Many investors were needed for such an undertaking. But, with Gil Green in charge, it was bound to be a success for the people and the village of Bird-In-Hand.

Gil continued as he faced the crowd, "But which one of the locals, an adult, is concealed inside this bird costume? Whoever can guess the identity of The Bird before Saturday, will receive a trip for four to Hersheypark, Hershey, Pennsylvania, and a one-hundred-dollar savings bond. And all it will cost you to guess is a donation of one dollar. Some of you are visitors to our area and don't want to guess the identity of our bird. That's okay. You can write your name and address on the slip of paper and donate your money. We will have a separate drawing for a second one-hundred-dollar savings bond for you folks. Thank you very much and have fun guessing."

Brian got all excited. "That's a great idea, but how did you know about it beforehand?" he asked when Sammy returned from picture taking.

"Gil Green was in the shop earlier this morning and told us. He wondered what we thought of the bird idea. He's also trying to get my parents to invest money in his Amish Virtual Reality project."

"Mr. Green is the perfect man to be in charge of this David Lapp fund-raiser," said Brian. "He comes up with some great ideas."

The tourists, who came to experience a slower, more relaxed way of life, had no idea who might be in the bird costume. However, they lined up with the rest of the locals to donate their money. Two lines formed around the platform as the contributors signed their names to slips of paper along with their guesses of The Bird's identity.

Suddenly, a small, middle-aged, and disheveled man moved unexpectedly from behind Sammy and Brian. He pushed his way through the crowd until he was next to the two young detectives. He faced the platform, strained his eyes as if to bring the scene into focus, and yelled, "Hey, I know who you are! You're . . ."

The man stopped and said no more. Instead he turned, swung his heavily tattooed arms into the air, and was face to face with the boys. "What do you think you're looking at?" He barked.

The two boys panicked! It was the man in the photograph, Chet Kelley's brother!

Chapter Two

The Bird looked out over the crowd as Gil Green urged the stranger to get in line, make his guess, and donate his money. But instead the man spun around and hurried away.

"What do you make of that?" asked Brian. "He isn't even from around here. How could he know who The Bird is?"

Sammy was still watching the tattooed man retreat, going west on Main Street. "He appeared to be confused. I wonder if he's aware his brother is trying to find him?"

Brian raised his eyebrows. "If he was my brother, I don't think I would want to find him." He gazed into Sammy's blue eyes. "Why do you think he ran away like that?"

"I have no idea," answered Sammy.

"Maybe he had to go to the rest room. Right, Sammy? Ha, ha!"

Sammy, missing the joke, pointed toward the long building. "If he needed a rest room, he could have gone into the Farmer's Market. Which reminds me, I'm hungry. How about you? Let's get a hot dog with sauerkraut."

A familiar voice filtered through the murmur of the tourists and village folks. "Sammy, Brian, looks like we have a good crowd."

The boys turned and saw Anne waving to them from the steps of the Little Book Shop. The shop, run by Anne, had once been a small, two-story, brick house. Now the building stocked thousands of new and used books.

"Yeah, business is booming," shouted Sammy. "Who's in the bird costume? If anybody knows, you should."

"You boys are the detectives. When you figure it out then you can tell me." Anne smiled and reentered her shop.

The two boys took one last glance at the feathered creature standing awkwardly on the platform, and then shuffled through some tourists toward the Farmer's Market.

In the summer of 1975, the Bird-In-Hand Farmer's Market property consisted of a brick house and a chicken hatchery. By the spring of 1976, a newly built, large white stucco building began operating as a farmer's market. Later, two outlets and the book store were added.

The meats, produce, baked goods, and crafts displayed at the market's many stands, attracted local patrons as well as tourists. Brenda's Snack Bar, a popular eating area, provided an adequate menu for the hungry visitors.

Sammy and Brian quickly claimed two seats when they became available at the snack bar. Sammy ordered his hot dog on a bun with the sauerkraut served separately on a small paper dish. Brian ordered the same.

"Well, what do you think?" asked Sammy between bites.

"About what?" Brian wondered what he had missed.

"Who do you think is wearing the bird suit?"

"Oh, that. I knew who it was right after Mr. Green made his speech."

Sammy knew by Brian's tone of voice what was coming, but he always welcomed Brian's game. "Okay, who?"

"Why someone from right here in Bird-In-Hand. Yep, one of our very own." Brian smiled and took another bite.

Sammy pointed and wiggled his finger. "Did you notice that someone is missing from behind the counter today?"

Brian glanced at the three teenagers taking orders and serving the food. "Yeah, Brenda isn't here." Brian brightened. "You think she's the one out there in the costume?"

"Not necessarily, but think about it. The person can't be in the bird costume and going about his usual business at the same time."

Brian was quiet for a time and then exclaimed, "So all we have to do is look around town to see who is missing. Right, Sammy?"

Sammy again used the plastic fork to stab at the sauerkraut on the paper plate. "That could certainly work, but it could take a lot of time."

"I guess so. But don't you see? We already know who The Bird is. Brenda!"

"Yes, can I help you?" came a familiar voice.

Brenda emerged from the stockroom at the far end of the counter. She was a small, slender woman in her forties with very short blond hair and a sparkle in her eye. "Oh, it's the super sleuths, Sammy and Brian. I read about your latest case in the newspapers. What can I do for you?"

Brian shook his head. "Oh, nothing. We were . . . just talking about you. Wondering . . . how many years you've been here in Bird-In-Hand."

Brenda pressed his lips together and looked up and to her right. "I've been here since B.T. Before Tourists."

Brian smiled. "That was back before I was born. Back in the old days."

"Which means, Brian," added Sammy, "Brenda has a lot more experience and wisdom than we do. We can learn a lot from her."

Brenda stood straight and watched the boys eat the last of their food. "Sammy's right, you know. I may be . . . ahem, middle age, but I'm still with it. Brian, let me ask you something. Do you know why Sammy asks for his sauerkraut on a plate instead of on the hot dog?"

"Sure," replied Brian. "He doesn't want the sauerkraut juice to soak the bun, just like me."

"But when you come in here by yourself and order, you always tell me to let the sauerkraut drain a little before I put it over the hot dog. Sammy could do the same. You see, Brian, Sammy knows the difference between the sauerkraut being on the hot dog and on the paper plate." Brenda glanced at Sammy and winked.

Brian shrugged. "I don't get it."

Brenda leaned closer to Brian and whispered, "You get more sauerkraut when we put it on the plate."

"As I said before, you are a very wise woman, Brenda," said Sammy.

Brenda stood tall and talked out of the side of her mouth. "If you ever need any help solving your mysteries, you know where I am."

As Brenda turned away to help other customers, Brian quietly asked Sammy, "Is that really why you ask for the sauerkraut on the plate?"

With a grin, Sammy swiveled off the stool and walked toward the exit. "What do you think?"

Brian followed. From then on, he would get the sauerkraut on the paper plate.

Outside, in the parking lot, people were still in line to donate their money for the fund-raiser. Several individuals surrounded The Bird, teasing it, and asking it questions. They were trying to get it to talk so they might recognize the voice or other mannerisms. But The Bird had been instructed not to talk or to make noises.

Sammy raised his camera and snapped a picture of The Bird reacting to the crowd. He had wanted to talk to Gil Green, but Gil was busy with three volunteers, collecting the paper slips and the money. Sammy obtained a pencil from one of the volunteers and pulled a small notebook from his pocket. He and Brian moved closer to The Bird.

"Now we're going to solve the mystery and win one hundred dollars. Right, Sammy?" said Brian.

Sammy was busy writing in his notebook. "First of all, we're not interested in winning any money. And second, right now we're only collecting facts that, when put together, will help us solve the mystery."

"Well, what are you writing? We don't have any clues yet."

Sammy closed the notebook. "I have two listed so far." And having said that, he crushed the paper napkin he brought from the snack bar, threw it at The Bird, and observed as The Bird swung at it with a wing. "Now I have three facts."

Brian watched as Sammy picked up the napkin and recorded fact number three. "Oh, Great One," Brian teased, "would you reveal to me your three sacred pieces of truth? I have traveled for miles and miles up and around this mountain, searching for you and the wisdom you possess." Brian bowed and tried to keep a straight face.

Sammy couldn't resist and replied, "Oh, seeker of truth, since you have abandoned your home and family and have traveled so far up this mountain to be at my side, I will reveal to you the three great truths that concern this mystery. Then you can ponder how you're going to collect three more great truths as you slide down the other side of the mountain."

"Was that a touch of humor I just detected?" asked Brian. "Am I finally rubbing off on you?"

"You just caught me at a weak moment. But, back to reality. How tall would you say The Bird is?"

Brian studied The Bird. "About five feet eight inches."

"I guess five feet seven inches. So there we have one fact. When I threw the napkin at The Bird, it reacted with its right wing, which could mean it's right handed. That's fact number two. And from the way the costume hangs, I'd guess the weight to be about one hundred forty pounds. Fact three." Sammy flipped the notebook closed. "Now, Brian, I'm going to let you collect the next three facts."

Before Brian could object, Norman Snyder, a local truck driver, and Buddy Kline, a recently laid-off factory worker, were arguing nearby. From what the boys could make out, Norman was reminding Buddy that his rent was past due. Buddy Kline rented a second floor apartment in a building on Main Street owned by Norman Snyder.

Quickly, Sammy's camera shot up and snapped a picture. He lowered the camera just in time.

Getting no money or satisfaction from Buddy, Norman turned and cornered the boys. "Hey, the guy's out of work. I know that, but he collects unemployment checks. Don't tell me he can't pay his rent."

Buddy Kline, who couldn't help but overhear the conversation, was very embarrassed and meekly walked away.

Norman moved in closer to the two boys, raised his hand, and shook his index finger. "I'll tell you what. This village is too small for what's going on here." He now shook his finger in the direction of the Bird in the Hand platform. "I don't like the idea of them making a spectacle here on Main Street with this fund-raiser thing. As if traffic isn't bad enough in this town. Does somebody have to be killed before something gets done about this mess? We already have outsiders roaming our streets and meddling into our affairs. And the Amish don't like it either. I'll tell you that."

Sammy didn't want to irritate Norman Snyder any more than he already was. "You're about right, Mr. Snyder. But there's nothing wrong with helping a neighbor when he's in trouble. And the tourists do bring money into the area which helps our economy. Don't you own a building and rent it out as store space?"

"Yeah, but I just own the building, not the business. Someone else will profit from the business venture." He pointed down the street. "Hey, your parents have a shop here. They're making the money. I'm a truck driver, delivering to the Amish farmers. I don't need the traffic mess that's here on Main Street. Do you know what it's like to be stuck in heavy traffic behind an Amish buggy with tourists running from one side of the street to the other? I tell you, someone's going to get themselves killed here. And it won't be hard for you boy detectives to figure out why."

Sammy was deep in thought as Norman marched over to Amos Stoltzfus, an Amishman, to restate his contempt for the carnival atmosphere and the "tourist pollution" in the town. Amos had heard these complaints before, even from his own people. But he was one of the new-trend Amish, the off-farm businessman. In recent years good farmland had become scarce and expensive, forcing the Amish into new kinds of manual work. Amos Stoltzfus profited from tourism by making and selling lawn furniture.

However, today, Amos was not making or selling lawn furniture. He was here at the fund-raiser because he and David Lapp were good friends who lived within the same church district. Amos had volunteered to take the donated money and apply it toward the purchase of lumber and hardware needed to rebuild the barn. The Amish community agreed that Amos was the man for the job.

Sammy watched as Norman Snyder left his compassionless listener. Amos approached the hustle and bustle around the Bird in the Hand platform. The Amishman wore a beard, a wide-brimmed straw hat, light-blue shirt, black cotton trousers with suspenders, and black work shoes. He looked up at the gaudy, red, yellow, and blue feathered bird costume and shook his head. Sammy noticed the many tourists staring at Amos because he was Amish. Then Sammy's sad blue eyes lowered as he wondered if the area really was becoming a theme park.

Brian interrupted the thought. "Well, are we going to donate our money and guess who's suffering in that elegant, feathered sweat suit, or are we going to collect more clues?"

"Let's go back to the shop and plan our strategy." Sammy turned, walked past The Little Book Shop, and continued toward the Bird-In-Hand Country Store.

Brian followed. "Why don't we just walk around town for a while to see who's missing? That way we'll have a couple of possible suspects to start with."

"A couple?" Sammy's voice was stern. "There's going to be hundreds of people we're not going to see."

Brian wanted so much to be like Sammy. Moments like this made him wonder if he was making any progress. Right then he made himself a promise. Regardless of the three clues Sammy already had, he, Brian, would be the one who would solve this mystery of *The Bird in the Hand.*

"Hey, Brian," said Sammy, "isn't that our tattooed friend going into our shop?"

Brian raised his hand to shade his eyes. "Yeah, and he's still alone. Let's see what he's up to."

The two boys hurried down the street and trailed Tattoo into the store. He had ignored the greeting from Mr. Wilson and headed straight for the quilt room. The boys followed but hung back by the doorway.

Not everyone who visited the quilt room came there with intentions of purchasing a quilt. Some tourists walked through to admire the art and needlework. Mrs. Wilson tried to identify the potential buyer from the "lookers" so she could provide the necessary assistance. "Are you interested in a quilt?" she asked.

Tattoo started to swing the metal arms of the quilt rack. "I might be." He moved to the bed covered with many Amish quilts and roughly grabbed at them to flip them back so they could be examined. A sign that rested on the top quilt, asking that the quilts not be touched, was flung to the floor.

Mrs. Wilson was annoyed. "We ask that you please not touch the quilts . . ."

"You what?" The stranger snapped the quilt corners back onto the bed.

Before the situation got out of hand, Mrs. Wilson glanced behind the man at her son. "Sammy, will you help me flip these quilts back so this gentleman can get a better look at them?"

The man turned and was face to face again with both boys.

Brian quickly sidestepped behind Sammy.

"Ain't I just seen you two up the street?" His face grimaced. "Are you two following me?"

"Oh, no," said Mrs. Wilson. "That's my son, Sammy, and his friend, Brian."

Before Tattoo could react, Sammy zipped around the man and lifted the bottom corner of the top quilt. His mother lifted the opposite corner, and together they folded back the quilt to display the next pattern beneath.

"Tell us when you see a quilt you like. Do you have a certain color and pattern in mind?" asked Sammy.

The stranger's faced relaxed as he thought about the question. "No, it's for my mother back home. I haven't seen her for years, and I want to buy something nice."

Sammy and his mother continued to turn back the quilts as Sammy said, "These are queen size quilts. An Amish woman sews the entire quilt by herself so the stitching will be uniform." Sammy paused and examined the white tag attached to the quilt's bottom edge. "This quilt took over seven hundred hours to make and costs six hundred fifty dollars. Which means the woman is making less than a dollar an hour." He was repeating what he had heard his mother say hundreds of times.

The stranger was not impressed. "Keep turning. I'll know it when I see it. There! Stop! That's the one I want. Mom likes stars."

"That's a popular design," said Mrs. Wilson. "It's called the 'Lone Star.' The quilting makes it appear as though light is radiating out from the main star in the center. And then, of course, you have the four stars that overlay the pillow area."

"I'll be back tomorrow to get it."

"You understand, we can't hold it for you. If . . ."

"Look, lady, I'll be back. I ain't got the dough now. But I'll have it by tomorrow."

Sammy thought he'd take a chance. "By what I heard you say up the street, you have a good opportunity to win a one-hundred-dollar savings bond and tickets to Hersheypark by winning the contest."

"A what?" He laughed. "By tomorrow I'll have enough dough to buy all the quilts in this room."

He turned to leave. Brian jumped aside to afford plenty of space for Tattoo to pass into the shop's main room.

"Oh, by the way," said Sammy, "a man was in here this morning looking for you. Had a picture. Said he was your brother."

"Really? Well, I ain't got no brother." He hurried toward the front door.

Sammy followed and stopped at the cash register counter where his father was busy with a customer. "Here, sir," said Sammy, "let me give you one of our business cards. You might be confused later by all you've looked at here. There are several shops with quilts like ours on Main Street. I'll write the name of the quilt pattern and the price on the back of the card for you."

The man paused as Sammy wrote the information and then handed him the business card.

"Here," said Brian, "take another card just in case."

The card was grabbed by the stranger but was still in Brian's hand when Brian quickly said, "Oh, I'm sorry. We're only allowed to give one card."

Brian jumped back, retaining the card as the stranger shook his head and stormed out of the shop.

Mrs. Wilson look puzzled. "What was that all about with the card, Brian?"

Brian's hand was still shaking as he held the card. He produced a wide grin and said, "I got his fingerprints."

"That's great," said Sammy. "That was smart thinking."

"It was?" said Brian.

"I know I'd be too scared to try something like that," said Sammy.

"You would?" Brian went into his brave act routine. "No, I wasn't scared at all. There was nothing to it. You know, there are times when you just have to stay calm and assert yourself." Brian handed the business card to Sammy as he danced from one foot to the other. "Do you mind if I use your rest room? I really have to go."

Sammy held the card by the edges as Brian hurried up the stairs to the bathroom. "Wouldn't it really be something if our stranger went out and robbed a bank?" Sammy said softly to no one in particular. He stepped back behind his sports card counter and inserted the business card into a plastic sleeve to protect the fingerprints in case they might be needed.

"Where do you think he's going to get all that money?" asked Brian when he returned from upstairs.

"I don't know," replied Sammy, "but I'm going to make a list. Where *does* someone, who's new in town, get his hands on a lot of money?"

"I bet number one on your list is, hold up a bank," said Brian.

"You read my mind," said Sammy. "What's number two on my mind?"

Brian shut his eyes and thought. "Kidnap somebody. Right, Sammy?"

Sammy was really thinking, sell something of value, but he didn't want to disappoint his friend. "Brian, how do you do it?"

Recovering from the shock, Brian said, "It's a gift. Yes, we selected few have special mind-reading powers that we obtain from the great beyond, and even beyond that. But I am too humble to tell you of the greatness I repress every day so that . . ."

Sammy grinned. "Enough, Brian, enough. I get the picture. So while I'm working on the mystery of the stranger, why don't you go and solve the mystery of The Bird by reading its mind?"

Chapter Three

By ten o'clock the next morning, the boys were helping to get the shop ready to open. The "quilt of the day" was displayed on the front porch along with other samples of Amish made crafts. When this was done, Sammy and Brian backed off the crowded porch and were instantly showered with bright sunlight. A warm breeze was making its way down Main Street which would soon be alive with tourists, flitting from one shop to another. Tourists were in season.

"Hey, boys, know who The Bird is yet?" yelled a voice from the shop across the street.

Sammy turned and squinted into the sunlight. He waved. "Hello, Mrs. Dagen. We're working on it."

"Yeah, we're working on it," repeated Brian, sidestepping to allow anxious tourists to enter the Bird-In-Hand Country Store.

"It's not my husband, I'll tell you that," shouted Mrs. Dagen. "You couldn't get him away from those soap operas for five minutes let alone five days." She shook her head, waved one hand at the ground, and disappeared into her shop.

"Sammy," said Brian, "I'm going to walk around town to look for clues. I want to see who I don't see. Because who I don't see might be who I can't see in the bird suit. You can see that, can't you, Sammy?" Brian displayed a wide grin.

Sammy took his best friend by the arm and pulled him closer. "And while you're at it, you might want to *see* why someone would want to appear in a bird costume for five days and perform for a crowd." He winked at Brian and gave him the thumbs-up.

Brian joined the herd of tourists headed toward the Bird-In-Hand Farmer's Market. "Who *would* want to wear a bird suit for five days, especially in this hot weather?" he muttered to himself.

Sammy wanted to concentrate on the mystery of the tattooed stranger and was glad when Gil Green spun out from a group of tourists.

"Morning, Sammy. I wanted to ask you, who was the man standing next to you yesterday who yelled that he knew The Bird?"

"According to a photograph I saw yesterday, he is supposed to be a Chet Kelley's brother," answered Sammy. "Why do you ask?"

"Oh, no reason," replied Gil Green. "I just thought it odd that, since he was a stranger, he would know who our bird might be."

"So you didn't know who the stranger was either?" asked Sammy.

"No, I sure didn't. You sure would remember someone with those tattoos. The tattooed snakes around his wrists gave me the creeps."

Sammy wondered why anyone would want to "spray paint" himself with a needle. He made a mental note to consult his psychology books. "The man, himself, gave me an odd feeling," stated Sammy. "I'm glad he didn't stay around too long. By the way, I suppose you know who is in the bird costume."

"That I do. I'm the only one who knows since I'm the one who made the arrangements with the person to wear the bird suit. However, I suspect by this time you also know. I've heard of your reputation as a detective."

"Brian and I are not ready to commit ourselves yet. We still have four more days so why rush?" Sammy glanced up Main Street in the direction of the market and noticed the crowd around the Bird in the Hand platform. "Looks like the contributions are still pouring in for the David Lapp fundraiser."

"The money we collect won't pay for all lumber and hardware needed to replace the barn, but it should be a substantial amount." Gil Green grabbed a card from his shirt pocket and frowned. "Well, I must leave to make a phone call."

Displaying a note of recognition, Sammy leaned forward for a better view. Something looked familiar. "Isn't that our store's business card you have there? You're standing in front of our store now; you don't have to phone. Just walk in."

"What?" Gil inspected the card. "Oh, yes, it is your card, isn't it." Gil Green turned the card around to show Sammy. "It's the number written on the back here that I have to call. But, I always keep your card handy to refer customers your way. We businessmen have to help each other, wouldn't you say?"

As Gil Green hurried away, Sammy had an odd feeling. He was about to re-enter the shop when he saw Chet Kelley standing next door in front of the post office. Sammy hurried inside the shop, grabbed his camera, and returned in time to get a picture. Kelley then quickly whirled around and headed down the alley beside the post office. Sammy followed and turned the corner in time to catch Kelley sneaking behind the building. He hurried and soon reached the end of the structure. Suddenly two strong arms reached out, grabbed him, and slammed him up against the back wall.

Chapter Four

"You country hicks are easy to trick," strained Chet Kelley, holding Sammy tight to the wall. "I knew you'd follow me back here. Right here where I wanted you. Now I know you and your friend saw my brother yesterday because I had a little talk with him this morning. My brother tells me he's getting his hands on a lot of money today. What I want you to tell me right now is, is it true? And if it is, where is he getting the money?"

Sammy was gazing into the face of a thug who could easily have killed or at least maimed hundreds of victims. He didn't want to be one of them. He decided the honest approach would be best. "It's true we ran into your brother twice yesterday."

Kelley released his grip on the boy and relaxed his face a little but kept Sammy pinned to the wall with his body.

Sammy continued, "We saw him at the fund-raiser, and then later he came into my parents' shop to look at quilts."

"The money! The money! What did he say about the money?"

"All he said at the shop was that by today, he would have money to buy a quilt. He didn't say where he was getting the money."

Kelley reluctantly backed away, and Sammy realized the threat was over. Spectators were gathering, curious about the commotion that was coming from behind the post office.

"Okay, don't do anything stupid. I believe you. Have a nice day," he said sarcastically and hustled away and quickly got lost in the crowd.

From his front bedroom window, Sammy could clearly see Main Street. Nine-thirty in the evening after all the shops were closed, the activity of the town didn't stop, it just wound down a bit. There was Norman Snyder's truck stuck behind an Amish buggy again. However, the compassion of the evening allowed the buggy to switch to the buggy lane so the truck could resume its normal speed. It was unusual for Norman Snyder to be working this late, thought Sammy as he watched the truck continue east on Main.

"I made a list of reasons people would want to be in the bird costume," said Brian, sitting on the edge of the bed.

Sammy turned from the window and walked over to his oak desk. "Good, let's hear it."

"Number one, someone owed Mr. Green a favor. The only person I can think of is David Lapp. I didn't see him at the fund-raiser. Did you?"

"No, but I doubt that David could be The Bird. He's too busy on his farm cleaning up after the fire. And besides, he's taller and heavier than The Bird."

"Number two," continued Brian, "likes to be in front of people. Anybody come to mind there?"

"Simon Witmer, the director of the dinner theater," said Sammy. "He loves to direct and act. He's about the right size, too."

"Well, let's see. Number three, someone wants to get away from home or job for five days. Now that could be anybody and everybody," said Brian frustrated.

"Maybe you're trying too hard. What did The Bird say? Did you get any thought vibrations?"

"Hey, that bird isn't talking. And birdbrains don't think. It just shook its head and patted the top of my mine with its wing." Brian flopped back on the bed with his arms under his head. "But I got some good suspects by snooping around. You know Jake Hess at the hardware store? He wasn't there. And get this. They said he wouldn't be in for a few days."

"And?" Sammy sat at his desk half listening to Brian, his mind still concentrated on Tattoo.

"Mary Witmer at the bake shop is on vacation. What do you think of that?"

"The bake shop, huh?"

"Yeah, well, I was hungry. All that concentration, trying to read The Bird's mind, used up all my energy."

"May I make a guess," said Sammy, "that you have donuts in the paper bag you have hidden in your sleeping bag?" Sammy stooped over and pulled back a portion of the cover, exposing the bag.

Brian pulled himself up on the bed. "Yep, they're for our midnight snack. Aren't you glad you have a friend like me?"

"I better say, yes, or you may not let me have that chocolate-covered donut I've been smelling all evening." Sammy lifted his nose into the air and took a deep breath. "Ahhhh."

"So that's how you knew about the bag of donuts."

Sammy's right hand changed into the shape of a gun and pointed directly at Brian. "If you want to be a good detective, you have to use *all* your senses."

Brian paused to make a mental note of that and then said, "Well, let's eat." He sprang from the bed and grabbed the bag of donuts. "I know it's early, but it has to be midnight somewhere in the world."

As the boys munched on the donuts, Sammy tried to made sense out of the stranger's irrational behavior. How could he possibly know The Bird? What was to be the source of the expected money? What was Mr. Kelley's involvement in all of this? Sammy knew there had to be a connection between the bird contest, the money, Mr. Kelley, and the tattooed stranger.

Brian couldn't stand the silence. "I shared my donuts with you. You want to share your thoughts with me?"

"I can't figure out our Mr. Tattoo," said Sammy as he wiped the last of the chocolate from his fingers. "He didn't return for the quilt today."

"I guess he doesn't have the money yet," said Brian. "No banks were robbed."

"Why is he in town? What is Chet Kelley's real connection to him? And what about the money? Where is it coming from? And last of all, Chet Kelley seems more interested in the money than in his so-called brother. He told me he had talked to his brother this morning. If that's true, why didn't his brother tell him where the money was coming from?"

"Sounds like they aren't too friendly," said Brian. "I bet Mr. Kelley wants the money for himself, the way he's going to a lot of trouble over it. You know, grabbing and pressuring you for information behind the post office."

"Maybe they really are brothers, and the one is trying to keep the other from getting into trouble. Chet might think, or even know, his brother is dealing in drugs or something."

Not to be outdone, Brian said, "Yeah, or how about this? The two were partners and they robbed a bank somewhere. They got separated somehow, and the one carrying the money ended up here and hid the money. The other guy trailed his friend here and now wants his half of the loot."

"Well, I don't know," answered Sammy. "But I do know, tomorrow morning we should make a trip to the police station and have a talk with our friend, Detective Ben Phillips. See if he knows anything about Chet Kelley."

Further discussions on this matter were interrupted as unexpected whining of sirens emerged from the street below. The boys raced to the front window in time to see the traffic part and allow two fire trucks to go east on Main.

"Hey, look!" yelled Brian as he pressed his face against the glass and peered right. "There's the fire! It's another Amish barn!"

Sammy could see the flames and black smoke that were ravaging the still and peaceful night air. Both boys stood frozen, fixated by the lure of the dancing flames and the mysticism of the dark smoke.

Brian finally broke the eerie silence. "Does this mean we're going to have another fund-raiser?"

Chapter Five

Detective Ben Phillips, six foot two, middle-aged, heavyset, with a thin mustache and a receding hairline, was not in the best of moods at nine o'clock Wednesday morning. He had been up most of the night on a developing case and was developing a headache as well. The arrival of Sammy and Brian, however, gave him an excuse to shift gears and relax a little.

He ushered them into his cubbyhole of an office and sat at his desk. He pointed to two folding chairs. For the teenagers, the office was like a home away from home. Or as Brian said, a closet away from home. They sat and faced the man who had become their best friend in the police department. The boys in the past had depended on him for assistance in solving some cases. Respect, confidence, and admiration developed between Detective Phillips and the boys as they relied on each other for answers.

Sammy didn't waste time in explaining their reason for being there. He revealed the details of Chet Kelley's search for his brother and the apparent importance of money. As he started to give a physical description of the men, the detective listened intently. But when Brian interrupted and made a reference to the man's tattooed arms, the detective sprang from his chair.

"This is incredible," he said. "Did you hear about the fire last night at Andy Beiler's place? A tobacco shed burned to the ground."

"Yeah, we saw it from Sammy's bedroom window," answered Brian.

"Well, in the ashes of that fire, the firemen found the remains of a badly burned body of a man. They immediately contacted the PSP and us."

"What's the PSP?" asked Brian.

"Oh, I'm sorry. The Pennsylvania State Police," said Phillips. "The only visible evidence of possible identification that was left in the ashes was teeth and a piece of tattooed skin. Luckily, because the corpse was lying on his left side, parts of the upper left arm were not entirely burned."

"And you don't know who he is or if the fire killed him?" asked Sammy.

"No. We're waiting for the medical examiner's report for the cause of death. We'll also try to identify the remains through dental records if it's at all possible. Keep in mind, he may not be *your* tattooed man."

"Hey, our man was supposed to stop by the shop yesterday to pick up a quilt," said Brian, "and he didn't show up."

"Yes, that's right!" continued Sammy. "Detective Phillips, I think you'll find that the tattooed man was killed before the fire was set."

"Well, we'll know for sure when we get the medical examiner's report."

"Would the fingerprints of our man help you out?" asked Sammy.

"You have fingerprints!? I don't believe it!"

Sammy explained the details of how Brian ob tained the fingerprints on the business card at the shop. Phillips immediately made arrangements to have the card picked up by a patrol car.

"Even if he is our man," said the detective, "we don't know if he was the one who started the fire, or even how he got there. The PSP checked for . . ."

"The Pennsylvania State Police," said Brian.

"Right. Actually, the Pennsylvania Fire Marshal, Lieutenant Arnold Thomas secured the area then carefully searched for the fire's origin. Casts were made of several tire tracks found in the loose dirt. I'm expecting to hear from him later today. And depending on what the medical report says, maybe we can round up this Chet Kelley character and get some answers."

"Do you think Kelley killed him and then took the money?" asked Brian.

"That's a possibility," said the detective, "*if* the corpse is your man."

"Oh, by the way," said Sammy, "who called in the fire alarm?"

Phillips consulted his folder. "Norman Snyder."

Sammy and Brian rode their bikes back to the shop and then walked up the street to the fund-raiser. This was the day the boys had decided to enter their guesses to The Bird's identity. They decided if new evidence was found and they changed their minds, another contribution and a new name could be entered.

As the two boys received their ballots and made a donation, The Bird was entertaining the crowd with its attempt at pantomiming. Having more experience, The Bird was now more outgoing as it shuffled from one end of the platform to the other. The two teenagers watched as The Bird hopped up and down. The crowd laughed. All the village needed now was a baseball team, thought Sammy sarcastically.

"Whose name are you going to enter?" asked Brian.

Sammy slid his notebook from his pocket, flipped it open, and reviewed his clues. "I don't want to influence your guess with mine. So suppose we both keep our entries a secret."

Brian got his notebook and flipped it open just as his friend had done. "Well, I was willing to share with you my scientific findings of the last few days," said Brian, going into his little act. "But if that's the way you want to treat me, okay, I can take it. The reason we've remained best friends over the years is that I've been willing to suffer in times like these. You have hurt me many, many times. I have suffered and bled for you just to keep our . . ."

"Brian, I'm not going to reveal my guess." Sammy wrote a name then his name and address, folded the paper, and handed it to the volunteer.

"Okay, then I'm not going to tell you mine. But did you know Jake Hess wasn't at the hardware store again today?" asked Brian as he wrote a name on his slip of paper.

Sammy smiled and pointed. "Maybe that's because he's on the other side of the platform helping to collect the slips and money."

Brian looked. Sure enough, Jake Hess was putting money into a large glass jar and ballots into a carton box.

"You didn't by any chance write Jake Hess's name on your paper, did you?" Sammy tilted his head and gave a half smile.

"Oh, no, no. He wasn't my only suspect. I have several more, you know." He pinched his lips together and frowned. "Do you have an eraser I can use?"

"Yeah, here you go." Sammy pretended to look elsewhere.

Brian erased the paper then slowly searched the crowd gathered in the Farmer's Market parking lot. He glanced at Sammy who was now watching him and then hesitated before he wrote. "How does the name Mary Witmer sound to you? She was missing from the bake shop again today."

Brian was anticipating hopeful signs as Sammy replied, "Sounds good to me."

He took that as words of encouragement as he wrote Mary's name on his paper and handed it to the volunteer.

"You might have a winner there," said Sammy.

Brian smiled and wondered, would this be the time he would outguess Sammy?

Sammy nudged Brian. "Look who's over there."

Eating a hot dog and leaning against his truck, was Norman Snyder. He was wearing worn cover-alls over a dirty undershirt. Norman had returned to town about a year ago and now lived with his mother. He invested money in a Main Street property which housed a business area on the first floor and an apartment overhead. His truck hauling business supplied additional income. Sammy noticed his work shoes and truck tires were covered with mud.

"You working in the mud these days, Mr. Snyder?" asked Sammy as the boys approached him.

"Yeah. I'm helping Andy Beiler. Terrible, terrible. Fire made a mess of his tobacco shed last night. They found a dead body after the fire. Burned up real bad."

"Lucky you were there when it started."

"What . . . what do you mean?"

"Detective Phillips told us you called in the alarm."

"Well, yes, I come along after it started. The shed was small, but that was the biggest blaze I'd seen in these parts. It went up fast. Too late when the firemen arrived. Too late. Yep, terrible, terrible." He shook his head and grabbed another bite of his hot dog and sauerkraut.

Brian was getting hungry. "You know, Mr. Snyder, you should ask for the sauerkraut . . ."

"People on the go don't have time for that, Brian," Sammy interrupted. Then he added, "Well, good luck with the cleanup, Mr. Snyder."

Instead of heading for the snack bar in the Farmer's Market, Sammy led his reluctant friend back toward The Bird. Seems strange, he thought, that Mr. Snyder just happened to be at the fire. He wondered where Mr. Snyder was when David Lapp's fire occurred.

People were still milling around the platform, watching Gil Green and The Bird performing for the good of the cause. Sammy smiled and waved at The Bird. The Bird waved back.

Brian looked toward the Farmer's Market. "I bet you're getting hungry by now. Right, Sammy? All that thinking and talking and walking we've been doing all morning. Really makes a person hungry."

Sammy continued to wave but glanced toward Brian who now projected an innocent, unconcerned look. "This might be the last time we'll see our friend in the bird suit. It's only proper we wave good-bye."

Brian executed a weak wave and muttered to himself, "I can't believe I'm waving bye-bye to a bird."

As The Bird and Gil Green acknowledged their actions, Sammy yelled, "Good luck!"

"Who are you talking to now, The Bird or Gil Green?" asked Brian.

"What?" asked Sammy in deep thought.

"Who were you saying good luck to, The Bird or Gil Green?"

Sammy hesitated. Suddenly the mystery pieces rearranged themselves and the picture became clear. "That, Brian, is the key to this whole puzzle. Who was talking to whom?"

"Good luck is the key, and who was talking to whom? I hate it when you sound like our English teacher." It irritated Brian every time his friend held back information. This was one of Sammy's weaknesses that Brian could find no humor in. "Since when did you, Sammy Wilson, base anything on luck? Never before did we ever solve a case based on good luck, only on facts and evidence. We never accuse anyone without evidence. How many times have you said that to me? Plenty."

"We have some investigating to do before we can accuse anyone," said Sammy. "And this bit of good luck tells us what we are going to do."

"Sammy," said Brian, making a move and in the beginning, playfully twisting Sammy's arm behind him, "I don't want the good luck to tell me anything." He twisted harder; he was mad now. "I just want you to tell me, and without riddles, what is it we are going to do?"

Sammy felt pain and replied, "Why, we're going to break into a house tonight."

Chapter Six

By eleven o'clock that night, the David Lapp open-air fund-raiser had been deserted for two hours. The Bird, Gil Green, David Lapp, Amos Stoltzfus, and all the volunteers had gone home. Hot air dusted over the empty Bird in the Hand platform. Two more days to go. Money was coming in generously. It would buy a lot of lumber and hardware for David Lapp's new barn.

And The Bird was home relaxing. It was out of uniform and wearing clean everyday clothes. The long shower earlier had washed away the sweat and the weariness. The Bird was losing weight. But that was all right, thought The Bird. It was worth it. The Bird had worked up an appetite. It was hungry.

Mercury street lamps cast an eerie blue security blanket over Main Street. An occasional metallic rumble, leather rustling, and horse hooves, announced the Amish buggies, claiming their road past civilization. A few tourists, trying to stretch out their vacation by cruising the night, watched as the buggies trekked by. Other tourists were safely isolated in motel rooms making their plans for the next day. Sammy, having obtained permission from his parents, had already made plans with Brian - for that night.

At eleven o'clock at night, the old, wooden, two-story building looked no different from the other old buildings on Main Street. The difference was, it was owned by Norman Snyder, truck driver. Norman wasn't one to keep his building maintained. But the Klines, who rented the apartment upstairs, found the rent reasonable so they tried not to complain. The bottom floor, which consisted of three rooms and a bath, had recently been rented to Gil Green for his soon-to-be-opened Amish Virtual Reality.

The rear of the building offered the young teenage detectives no kind welcome as they groped in the darkness. They pressed their faces to a window. "Hey, it's dark in there," whispered Brian. "Nobody's home. Let's go."

Sammy patted his friend on the shoulder. "Now, wait, Brian. Take it easy. We're searching for clues, and they can be lying around in the dark."

He took another look around before he slipped over to the rear door and tried the knob. It was unlocked! "Brian, we're in luck," he said softly as he slowly opened the door, listened, and then stepped inside.

From the puzzle pieces Sammy had collected thus far, he felt this business operation somehow had a connection to the mysterious tattooed man. Normally he wouldn't resort to late-night surveillances or to putting himself and his best friend in danger. However, from what he suspected, he calculated that tonight the risk would be small.

"W-What if Mr. Green finds out about us? W-We're breaking the law," stammered Brian as he hurried to follow his partner into the building. "What then?" Brian loved playing detective, but he wasn't exactly enjoying it at the moment.

"We found the door unlocked didn't we? We're investigating a possible break-in. Trust me." Sammy carefully closed the back door, and the two teenagers stepped further into the dark room. "We won't get into trouble. In fact we'll be doing a lot of good."

As soon as Brian heard the words "trust me," he relaxed a little. He knew from experience Sammy didn't use those words lightly. If only he could reach the level where Sammy could put as much trust in him.

"What if somebody's here?" whispered Brian. "I think I hear something."

Some stray light from the room ahead revealed that the room was not empty. Without warning, Brian bumped into a tall mass that moved, knocked him down, and fell on top of them. "Help! Help! Get off of me!"

Sammy jumped aside, ready for action. He saw no one. No movement. "Are you all right, Brian?" he asked, trying to stay on his feet the best he could in the darkness.

"Somebody's attacking me," muttered Brian. "Get him off of me!"

Sammy followed Brian's voice, felt his arm, and pulled him out from under something. "It's okay. We're alone. I think."

"I hear noises," answered Brian. "It's all around us."

Their security slightly shaken, the boys thought it wise to use their small flashlights which they slid from their pockets. As their tiny beams of light swept across the floor, they discovered they had been attacked by a pile of empty carton boxes.

They were surprised to find the room bare except for two piles of boxes plus the defenseless cartons that were victims of the darkness. But the room seemed to come alive. The sounds persisted. Ghostly noises came from everywhere. The bare walls seemed to echo every sound that had ever disturbed their surfaces.

Sammy grinned as he watched Brian's fear displayed and emphasized in the jerky movements of his flashlight beam.

"Are . . . yoooou scared, Sammy?" slurred Brian, his voice changing an octave higher.

"No," answered Sammy. "Are you?"

"Nooo, it's just that I don't like to talk to strangers."

"Why, are you hearing voices?"

"I'd rather not." Brian's hazel eyes opened wide as he moved closer to his friend and quickly scanned every corner of the room.

"You want to leave?"

"Yeah. The way I figure it, there's only room in here for the two of us."

Sammy smiled, "Now come on. You know it's only the creaking bones of an old house you're hearing."

"I don't mind when a house creaks, but I don't like it when it cracks its knuckles." Brian shivered and closed his eyes — but only for a split second.

"Get serious," said Sammy. "We better restack these boxes. No need for anyone to know we were here."

They crept slowly past the rebuilt stack of cartons and snuck into the front room. Narrow slits of dim, blue light crept in through the side of each window shade, producing mysterious shadows. This room, too, was bare except for the shadows, a telephone on a small metal desk, a chair, and more piles of cardboard boxes. As the boys centered their lights on several boxes, the markings showed they contained electronic components. The place looked the way they imagined a developing business would appear. It was waiting to be converted into the newest tourist attraction.

A faint noise seeped in from the room they had just left.

"Did you hear that?" whispered Brian.

"Yeah, it sounded like someone came in the back door," said Sammy. "Quick, hide behind the boxes, and turn off your light."

The stacks of cartons were high enough to conceal both boys. But just to make sure, Brian also hid behind Sammy.

The boys waited. Nothing. Except slight noises from the apartment upstairs. They waited some more. They listened. Just normal, occasional traffic outside on Main Street. Nothing else. Then . . . footsteps. Coming from the back room. Now entering the front room. Now . . .

Sammy slowly slid his face along the boxes to get a peek at the intruder. His left eye extended one inch beyond the edge. He couldn't believe what he saw. It was The Bird. And The Bird was holding a gun pointed toward them.

Chapter Seven

With its free wing, The Bird snapped on the lights, circled around the boxes, and faced the young boys. With several maneuvers, it indicated with the gun that the boys were to lie down on the floor on their stomachs.

Brian was shaking and the first to hug the floor. Sammy slowly sank to the floor. On his way down he took notice of the costume and the shoes. It was the same bird costume except for the feet. Now The Bird was wearing shoes instead of sneakers.

A heavy foot clamped down on Sammy's right shoulder, forcing his nose to the floor. As Sammy turned his face to his right, he picked up a familiar scent. The strong, strange smell was coming from the shoe planted on his shoulder.

The Bird pulled back on Sammy's arms and taped his wrists behind his back, entrapping some loose feathers along the way. He did the same with

Sammy's ankles. Small pieces of tape were applied across Sammy's eyes and mouth. Then The Bird repeated the same process with Brian, leaving the boys helpless on their stomachs.

Sammy concentrated now on every sound, listening for clues. Boxes were being moved and ripped open. He heard The Bird walking to the back door area and then returning. More boxes were moved and ripped open. More walking and returning. The last sound Sammy heard was the back door closing. And then nothing. Nothing at all. Except, music filtering from the apartment upstairs. Mixing with the distant noise of buggies and cars, interrupting the night and the little village of Bird-In-Hand.

Sammy squirmed and rolled until he reached Brian. His partner shook and jabbed his right elbow into his stomach. Sammy slid down until his face was touching Brian's taped wrists. Brian got the idea and moved his hands over Sammy's face until his fingers could seize the edge of the tape. Sammy rolled away, leaving the tape in Brian's hand.

"That's it, Brian," said Sammy now that his mouth was uncovered. "I'll roll back and you grab the tape on my eyes."

"Hello, anybody here?" called a voice from the darkness.

The boys froze. Listening. The voice came closer.

"Hello, anybody here?" the voice repeated. "It's Amos Stoltzfus."

"Yeah, over here," shouted Sammy, wondering what the Amishman was doing here this time of night.

Because the light was still on, Amos had no difficulty freeing the boys from their bonds. As soon as the tape was eased from Sammy's eyes and they adjusted to the light, he found the place a mess. The carton boxes, which covered most of the floor, had been cut open and emptied.

"What are you doing here, Mr. Stoltzfus?" asked Sammy as he helped Amos untape Brian's face.

Before Amos could answer, Brian put his hands to his face and asked, "Did the plastic surgery work? Are the scars and wrinkles gone? Am I young and handsome?"

Amos was shocked and shook his head at Brian's wit which was a foreign language to him. How could the "English" teenager make a joke out of a very serious situation? But Sammy understood. He knew that Brian's way of dealing with stressful situations was with humor. Try as hard as he could, Sammy could not express humor naturally. But then, he didn't have to. He had Brian as his best friend.

"You wouldn't have looked too handsome if I come in here oncest and found you shot yet," announced Amos, trying to re-establish the seriousness of the situation. "It wonders me how you got in this fix."

Sammy started to relate what had happened when someone unlocked the front door and walked in. It was Gil Green. "What's going on here? I saw lights . . . Oh, my . . . I've been robbed!" he yelled, seeing the many empty boxes scattered about. "Who did this?"

Sammy and Brian explained how they had found the back door unlocked, investigated, and had been overpowered by someone in the bird costume with a gun.

"After he bound us with tape," offered Brian, "he opened your boxes and carried the computer stuff out the back door. Is that the way you heard it, Sammy?"

"Something like that."

"There was a quarter of a million dollars worth of computer technology in those boxes," said Gil, turning some boxes over and inspecting inside. "I just made arrangements to have it all assembled, tested, and ready to open the front door for business."

"Did you have your equipment insured, Mr. Green?" asked Sammy.

"Oh, yes. The papers are there on my desk." Gil's blueish-gray eyes were sad. "The computer electronics can be replaced, but it will delay the grand opening." He kicked at the empty boxes and headed for the back door, stopping first to turn on the back light.

"Oh, one other thing," said Gil to the other three who had followed him to the back room. "The bird costume was in the bathroom, and I can see it's still there on the floor."

Sammy hurried and glanced at the costume that was lying carelessly on the floor. "Yes, this is the one. But, Mr. Green, how did the costume get here in the first place?"

"You know the Bird in the Hand contest was my idea. I enlisted one of Bird-In-Hand's own to wear the bird suit for the five days of the fund-raiser. Well, this building was the drop-off point. The person would come here in the morning, change into the costume, then be driven up to the display platform as The Bird. In the early evening The Bird would be driven back here, change in the bathroom, and then leave by this back door."

"So," interrupted Sammy, "the person wearing the costume took it off earlier this evening, left it here, and then went home."

"Right," replied Gil.

"Who locked the back door this evening?" continued Sammy.

"The door should have been locked by the person who left after taking off the suit. What are you suggesting?"

"Nothing," said Sammy, then added, "It's just that the door was unlocked when Brian and I were here at eleven o'clock."

Gil looked hard at Sammy. "Are you saying the person might have forgotten to lock the door?"

Sammy again examined the door and its lock. "I don't see any signs of forced entry. So either it was left unlocked or someone used a key to get in."

"Or," said Brian, "the mystery person who is The Bird, is also our mystery burglar. That person has been coming in here for three days. He sees all this valuable electronic equipment and decides to compensate himself for services rendered in the fund-raiser."

Gil responded to Brian's theory. "No, I think you're wrong."

"Can't you tell us who The Bird is?" asked Brian. "The fund-raiser is almost over. Just two more days. Who is it?"

"Sorry, the fund-raiser is not officially over until Friday evening. You'll have to wait until Saturday at one o'clock like everyone else," said Gil. "On Saturday, up at the stage, The Bird will be unmasked. We'll also announce the total amount of money collected for David Lapp."

Sammy was now convinced he had enough puzzle pieces to know the direction this mystery was heading. Another important piece of the puzzle, thought Sammy, would be the answer to a question. Why was Amos Stoltzfus here at this building tonight? Amos had appeared uneasy at the statement Gil had just made.

"Maybe somebody came in before you boys and wanted to steal this scientific stuff," said Amos. "And you interrupted him so he hid yet in the bathroom. Then he puts this here costume on oncest so his face ain't."

"There's one thing wrong with that, Mr. Stoltzfus," said Sammy. "Whoever took the computer equipment would need something to haul it away. Brian and I didn't notice any vehicles around the building when we arrived."

Amos smiled, "I should think before I say. That's why I'm a dumb Amishman and you boys are the detectives."

"Why, Mr. Stoltzfus," said Brian, "you do have a sense of humor."

"And, Mr. Stoltzfus," said Sammy, "I've seen the creativity and craftsmanship you put into your lawn furniture. And the size of your business tells me you're a very skilled and *smart* Amishman."

By this time Gil had opened the back door and was headed out. "Let's check if any trucks or vans arrived after you boys got here."

The three followed Gil Green outside and caught up with him at the stone alleyway that ran behind the building and parallel to Main Street.

"Nothing here now," said Amos, "except those tire tracks and dried pieces of mud."

Sammy carefully inspected the alleyway and then said, "Mr. Green, shouldn't you call the police and report the break-in?"

After the police arrived and Sammy and Brian had given their statements, they were allowed to leave. Sammy had hoped Detective Phillips would be in charge of this investigation. Since he was not, he and Brian would try to talk with him in the morning.

The boys hurried along Main Street because Sammy realized his parents would be worried about them if they didn't return home soon.

Sammy glanced down the street and noticed something he wanted his friend to see. "Hey, Brian, you can see your house from here."

"I think there's a light on in my house!" said Brian as he tried to fight off the fatigue due to the stress of the night.

Sammy, who was anxious to get home, said, "Maybe your parents are home early. You can check on it in the morning. Come on."

As the boys headed back toward the shop and much needed sleep, they caught their little village of Bird-In-Hand off guard. The absence of tourists and heavy traffic gave the small village a refreshing change of pace. Little Bird-In-Hand was claiming its well-earned time for calm, peaceful slumber. It was as if the village was catching its breath, recharging its batteries, until early in the morning when someone would flip the "on" switch.

Detective Phillips met his young friends in his office at ten o'clock in the morning. He stood behind his desk and looked at the two eager boys who had claimed their folding chairs. He shook his head and wished for the curiosity and energy of youth. The folder he was holding belonged to Detective Marvin Wetzel. "This report says that you boys were witnesses to a burglary last night. Got taped up by a bird or something like that. Sounds like an interesting case. Detective Wetzel is in charge of it. He's the officer you gave the information to last night."

"Seemed like a nice guy," said Brian, and Sammy nodded in agreement.

"Now, how about the fingerprints, any luck?" asked Sammy.

Phillips laid the folder on his desk and picked up another folder that bore his name. "The fingerprints we got off your business card and the dental plates found in the fire *are* from the same person," announced Detective Phillips. "And thanks to Brian here, the prints he got were identified as those of ex-con, Victor Marsh, a recent resident of the New York State Prison. The prison's dental records identified the dental plates and teeth as belonging to the same Victor Marsh." Phillips opened the folder and skimmed Marsh's record. "From what I see here, he was a small-time hood. Gambling was his weakness, always losing, always borrowing from the loan sharks, hoping to make that one big score. He ended up driving the getaway car in a bank job in New York, got caught, and spent four years in jail. Victor got out last month."

"And then for some reason, he decided to come our way," said Sammy. "But, why? The only thing we have to offer here is a good time for tourists."

"Maybe that's it," said Brian. "He came to see the Amish and to buy a quilt for his mother."

"I think it's more than that, Brian." Sammy pointed to the folder the detective was holding. "Did he have any relatives in the area?" asked Sammy.

Phillips consulted the records and after a few moments, shook his head and said, "No, nothing mentioned. His relatives seem to live in New York and New Jersey. His mother lives in New Jersey with her sister. There's one sister, married, living in Virginia."

"Where does his brother live?" asked Sammy.

The detective made another check of the folder and its papers and again shook his head. "No brother. He had no brother."

"Which brings us to, who is Chet Kelley?" asked Sammy. "And why was he only interested in money when he met and talked to Victor Marsh?"

"Maybe my idea was right, Sammy," said Brian. "The two of them robbed a bank, and Victor ran with the loot and hid it."

"Nope," said the detective, referring to his papers, "all the money from the bank job was recovered. And Chet Kelley was not involved in the robbery."

"But, money appears to be the connection between Kelley and Marsh," suggested Sammy.

Phillips picked up a note from the desk. "And another bit of information I received a little while ago. The fire is listed as arson."

"Yeah?" said Brian. "How do they know that?"

The detective reviewed the notes he had taken over the phone from the Fire Marshal. "Fire was started in two places. Some kerosene was taken from the heater and thrown over wood on the opposite wall. The kerosene heater was then knocked over to make it look like an accident. A match was used to ignite the wood on his way out of the shed." Phillips looked up from his notes and added with emphasis, "The same method used to torch David Lapp's barn."

"Really?" stated Brian. "That doesn't make sense."

"It might," said Sammy. "Who would benefit from the torching of Mr. Lapp's barn *and* the torching of Mr. Beiler's tobacco shed?"

"With Mr. Beiler, they wanted to get rid of Victor Marsh," said Brian.

Sammy pointed a finger at Brian. "Let's go one step further. They or he wanted the body destroyed beyond recognition."

"It sounds about right," said Phillips. "There were traces of kerosene found on the corpse. So who *would* gain from destroying Lapp's barn *and* having a body show up that couldn't be identified?"

Sammy cast hopeful blue eyes toward Phillips. "I might have a way to find out. Is it possible for you to fax a photograph to the warden at the New York State Prison?"

"Yeah, I can do that. What do you have on your devious mind now, Sammy?" He glanced at Brian as if to expect an answer, but Brian just raised his eyebrows and shrugged his shoulders.

The envelope Sammy was carrying contained four photographs, compliments of a one-hour process photo lab. He opened the envelope, selected two pictures, and handed them to Phillips. "See if the warden recognizes any of these men."

Phillips glanced at the photos, and with a quizzical look replied, "Sammy, why do I have the feeling you and Brian are going to solve this case for me?"

"Well, I don't know about that," said the teenager, "but we'll try."

"Solve this case," said Phillips, waving his folder, "and you can help Detective Wetzel with his." With his other hand Phillips grabbed the other folder and held them both in front of him.

"If I were you," said Sammy, "I'd put the two folders together. I think we're going to find they're both the same case."

Chapter Eight

"I don't mind telling you, I was scared," said Brian while the young detectives were pedaling east on Main. "I thought for sure The Bird was going to shoot us in the back when we were on the floor. Somcone sure doesn't want Mr. Green's Amish Virtual Reality to become a reality."

"Didn't something seem strange to you about the taking of the computer equipment?" asked Sammy.

His friend didn't answer right away. He was struggling to stay abreast with Sammy. "Oh, you mean, the person who did it must have had a key to the back door."

"No. Why didn't the thief leave the equipment in the carton boxes? It would be quicker and less complicated to load and haul it."

"I have a simple explanation for that," replied Brian, even surprising himself when he thought of it. "Did you notice the size of some of those boxes? Some of that equipment was probably too heavy to carry. He cut the tape, took out one piece at a time, and carried what he could in one trip. Right, Sammy?"

"Brian, I must admit I never thought of that," said Sammy truthfully. Of course he wasn't going to admit to his sidekick that his own theory was more likely. The fact that the thief found it necessary to put on the bird costume meant he was someone they knew. But when did he enter the building? Was he there before or after he and Brian had arrived? What about the back door?

"Maybe you can help me out with something else I'm having trouble with," said Sammy, knowing his friend would rise to the occasion. "Why was the back door unlocked when we got there?"

"I find that rather easy to answer," mused Brian. "In fact, I'm surprised you would ask such a question. Up to this very moment, I've held you in high esteem. But now . . ."

"Brian, I'm sorry, your time is up. Answer the question." Because the traffic was heavy, Sammy allowed Brian to pull ahead on his bike.

"What do I win if I answer your question?" shouted Brian over his shoulder.

"I will tell you a secret," yelled Sammy.

"Sounds good to me." Brian slowed down, allowing his friend to catch up. "Okay, the door was unlocked because the thief was already inside when we got there. How's that? What's the secret?"

"Then why," asked Sammy, "didn't we see his car, van or truck parked nearby? No, whoever he was, he came between the time we got there and the arrival of Amos Stoltzfus."

Brian picked up speed. "I guess I'm no help to you anymore," he teased. "So now I'm going home to my mommy and daddy. *They* appreciate me."

"But your mommy and daddy can't tell you the secret I know."

Brian's bike coasted for a while and allowed Sammy to catch up. "Okay, what's this big secret?"

"We're being followed by a dark-blue Ford."

Brian's bike started to wobble. He pulled over and almost stopped.

"Don't look around," his friend cautioned. "Let's just casually stop in that driveway and keep talking to each other and see what happens."

The boys entered the driveway, got off their bikes, and kept talking.

From the corner of his eye, Sammy saw the Ford had pulled over and stopped on the shoulder of the road, otherwise known as the buggy lane.

"Who is it?" asked Brian, trying to act casual while looking away from the car.

"I didn't see, but I believe he followed us from the station."

Brian couldn't control himself any longer. He turned his head and looked directly at the dark-blue Ford. Light reflected off the windshield, protecting the driver's identity and increasing the developing danger.

Suddenly the motor roared and the car sprang forward into the driveway, increasing its speed as it approached the young detectives.

The boys pushed their bikes further into the driveway.

The car kept coming.

Closer.

They threw their bikes down and ran toward the house.

The car stopped just short of running over the bikes. A large man emerged from the car and yelled after them, "It's okay, boys, it's me, Chet Kelley."

"What's he mean, it's okay?" said a winded and scared Brian Helm.

Sammy turned and faced Kelley while speaking to his friend. "Look, he's *not* going to hurt us. There's too much traffic here."

Kelley came closer. "I just want to ask some questions. What did the police have to say to you? Do they know who killed my brother?"

"How did you know he was killed?" asked Sammy.

"And he's not your brother," added Brian, bravely. "His name is Victor Marsh." Knowing the truth, gave Brian a sense of power over Kelley.

"You're right. He ain't my brother. But Victor would not be stupid enough to walk into a fire, sit down, and let himself be burned to death. I know Victor. He's stupid enough to get some bones broken but not to kill himself."

"All the police know at this time is a body was found in the fire," said Sammy. "They don't know if it was the fire that killed him. But they do know his name is Victor Marsh. That's it. If you know more than what I've just said, I suggest you go to the station and have a talk with Detective Phillips."

"Yeah, I'll do that," Kelley said with a tone that meant it would never happen.

Sammy wanted this man to go away, but he had to ask, "Did you ever find out where he was going to get the money?"

"No."

"Who are you really?" asked Brian. "How do you fit into all of this?"

Sammy winced. He didn't know if Brian was brazen or naive when he acted like this.

Kelley gave Brian a long, hard look, then lowered his gaze, turned and walked back to the Ford. Before he entered his car, he gave the boys one last look. "I suggest you kids go to the mall or watch television like normal brats. Stop wasting my time. Oh, and a word of advice, never borrow money from a loan shark." The dark-blue Ford, bearing a New York license plate, backed up and headed east on Main Street.

"Do you think that's what he was, Sammy? A loan shark?" asked Brian as the boys returned and inspected their bikes.

"Could be. Sometimes people need money so badly they are forced to borrow at high interest rates. And if they can't meet their payments, they end up with broken bones."

"Yeah, or even roasted in a fire. Right, Sammy?"

"No, not really. You see, if a lone shark breaks bones, he gets his money back plus a whole lot of interest. If he kills someone, he loses his money and the interest."

"Hey, I'm hungry," said Brian, jumping onto his bike. "How about a hot dog with sauerkraut?"

"Good idea," replied Sammy. He mounted his bike and headed for the road. Both boys turned right, going east on Main. Sammy quickly took the lead.

"That's okay!" yelled Brian. "First one there buys!"

Five minutes later as the boys passed the Bird-In-Hand Country Store on their way to the Farmer's

Market, they spotted Norman Snyder. He had just gotten out of his delivery truck and was headed for his building that housed Gil Green's Amish Virtual Reality on the ground floor.

The young detectives stopped, dismounted their bikes, and watched as Norman disappeared behind the building.

Sammy pulled his bike up onto the sidewalk. "Let's wait and see what he does."

Brian raised his bike and parked it next to Sammy's. "What do you expect him to do?"

"I have no idea."

Brian was disappointed. He had expected a more mind-boggling reply than that. "I can smell the hot dogs and sauerkraut from here. You too. Right, Sammy?"

"Let's feed our curiosity first," said Sammy.

Brian smiled. That, thought Brian, was a more commendable comment, worthy of his good friend.

It wasn't long until both Norman Snyder and Buddy Kline returned to the truck and drove off.

"Why are those two together?" asked Brian.

"Maybe Mr. Snyder is trying to collect some rent," suggested Sammy.

"Yeah, take Mr. Kline out into the country to break some bones."

Sammy waved his hand. "Come on, let's tail them."

Keeping up with the truck wasn't too difficult for the boys. Several Amish buggies took the zip out of the trip, giving the roaming tourists a sporting chance when crossing Main Street. However, further east, after the truck and the bikes passed the Farmer's Market and the Bird-In-Hand Restaurant, traffic would speed up, giving the young detectives a real challenge. They knew their bikes would be no match for the truck. It would be muscle power against horse power, and they would lose.

Pretty soon the truck appeared to shrink, getting smaller and smaller . . . and then it turned left heading north. The boys eventually did the same, but it was a losing battle. The truck had disappeared.

Sammy suggested they keep going for a while, hoping the truck might stop along the way somewhere.

Brian's stomach was telling him to turn back before he ran out of fuel. He needed a fill-up of hot dogs and sauerkraut. Sammy was a good friend, but how much does friendship count when a guy is really hungry?

"There," said Sammy, pointing. "Up the lane there. See the truck near the farmhouse?"

The truck appeared empty as the teenagers laid their bikes down in some bushes along the lane.

They crept closer, trying to hide themselves behind the truck away from the farmhouse.

"I don't see them anywhere. They must be in the house," said Sammy.

Brian didn't appreciate having a truck in front of his face. He had never examined a truck this close before. "I wonder what's inside this thing."

"Let's find out, but be careful," instructed Sammy.

Both boys crept slowly to the rear and inspected the tailgate. "I can see how to open the door," said Brian. "Shall we try it?"

"Yeah, but be fast. We don't know when the men will be back."

After Brian pushed in and raised a bar, the right, back door swung open and permitted the light to enter the otherwise pitch-black interior.

"Hey, there are wooden boxes in there," said Sammy as he climbed inside.

Brian followed, heaving himself up with Sammy's help. Many occasions served to remind Brian of his shortness. This was one, and it embarrassed him. He remembered the time in school when the gym teacher lined up the students according to their height. He was at the end of the line. Of course with his humor he didn't see it that way. He was first in line. The tall guy down the line was really at the end.

Sammy turned and examined the boxes. "There must be about fifteen or twenty wooden crates here. They look broken."

The boys heard a noise behind them. Before they could turn around, however, the truck's rear metal door clamored shut. Total darkness engulfed them. It was metal against metal as the outside bar was slammed down to lock them inside. They were trapped.

Chapter Nine

The swiftness of the unexpected action over whelmed the young detectives. They groped in the dark, heading for the back doors of the truck. They pushed against the metal wall and yelled. No response. Again and again they tried. Nothing. Then they stopped.

The intense, built-up August heat inside the closed truck and their spent energy forced the boys to sit and rest. They needed to regain their strength. They wanted to be ready for whatever happened next.

Suddenly the boys heard muffled voices. They sat still and waited. The truck's cab doors opened and shut. The motor sounded and the truck backed up, throwing the boys forward. As the truck turned and bolted straight ahead, the teen-agers were flung against the rear doors.

"You hurt?" asked Sammy. It was strange and scary being handicapped by the darkness.

"Yeah, my right arm is broken in three places. But, that's okay, I can set the bones myself," kidded Brian. With a change in attitude, he asked, "What about our bikes?"

"What about us? Hey, we can always come back for the bikes."

"If we survive this," added Brian. "Boy, am I hungry."

The truck made a left turn and later a right. About three minutes later, it turned right and then made a left and stopped.

Brian could feel the sweat invading his eyes, nose, and mouth and then dripping down into the darkness. "Wow, it's like an oven in here!"

"Yeah," said Sammy, "I was just thinking of the person wearing the heavy bird suit, all those feathers. He must be losing a lot of weight."

Suddenly for Brian, thoughts, like drifting sand, were escaping from the darkness. The thoughts came together and made sense. And then he believed he understood the secret. He knew about The Bird, and he smiled to himself. The sound of slamming doors brought him back to his present reality.

"What now?" asked Sammy as the boys started to hear faint voices again. He started to pound on the side of the truck. "I think we better demand some attention. Hey, let us out!"

Without warning, someone unlocked the back door, and it swung open.

"*Wow!*" proclaimed Brian as the boys blinked to ward off the overwhelming light.

"What are you two doing in there?" Norman Snyder looked surprised and very annoyed.

"Someone shut the door and locked us in," said Sammy.

"What were you two doing in my truck in the first place?"

Without hesitation, Brian said, "We were riding our bikes along the road, and we saw this guy opening the back doors of your truck. So we . . . we rode our bikes up the lane to get a closer look. The stranger threw . . . something into the truck, so we got closer. He saw us then ran away. We didn't see you around anywhere, so we . . . we got into the truck to see what was happening and . . . and the guy comes back and locks us in."

"Okay, get down from there," Norman ordered.

When the boys jumped off the truck, they noticed Buddy Kline standing to the side. They also realized they were standing in the alleyway behind Norman Snyder's property.

Norman inspected his truck. "I don't see anything in there other than my boxes." He glanced at both boys. "It can be very dangerous butting into other people's business. You could have been killed. Remember that. It's terrible, terrible. All right, you'd better go."

With perspiration-covered bodies and wet clothing, the boys hustled away without any hesitation. Brian was willing to forget the whole matter. The main item on his much relieved mind now was food, more specifically, hot dogs and sauerkraut. But, Sammy was not willing to forget. Since the details of the improvised truck experience did not compute with his already collected facts, new questions developed.

Without speaking, both boys knew they were headed for the Farmer's Market. Brian was wondering whether he should order two or three hot dogs. Sammy was creating questions. Why did Mr. Snyder meet with Mr. Kline and take him to an Amish farm? Whose farm was it? What took place in the farmhouse? Who locked them inside the truck? and why?

His sidekick added one more question. "How many hot dogs are you going to order?"

"What?" asked Sammy, ascending from deep thought.

"How many hot dogs are you going to eat? I'm going to eat three, with sauerkraut on the side."

"Why don't you start with one and then go from there?" suggested Sammy.

"That's a great idea," said Brian. "That way they'll stay hot. Right, Sammy?"

That wasn't what his friend had in mind. "So this *guy* comes along, opens the truck, and throws something inside, huh?" kidded Sammy.

"Yeah, how'd you like my story? Not bad for a modest, cute, and near-death-from-hunger, short boy with curly hair. Right, Sammy?"

Sammy smiled and shook his head. "Maybe you *should* eat three hot dogs."

The next day, the Bird-In-Hand Country Store's front porch was already dressed in antiques, Amish handicrafts, and a quilt rack, blooming with dahlias, when the doors opened at ten o'clock. Brian, carrying the morning paper, approached the porch several minutes later. He was bringing the paper for Mr. Wilson who liked to keep up on local events. The meandering of tourists over the porch and in and out the front door, made it difficult for Brian to have a direct shot for his grand entrance. So instead, he decided to infiltrate the tourists and go with the flow. He would eventually end up somewhere in the shop.

Sammy Wilson's sports cards counter was especially popular with young children who were visitors to the area. For them, nothing matched the excitement of going into a strange store in a strange town and finding that rare card needed to complete their set. Even the local Amish youths took their turn gazing at the selection of cards. They seemed to have the same interest in professional sports as "English" children.

Sammy was not surprised when an unexpected face popped up among the other five at the counter. "Hi, excuse me, but do you have any really old Ted Williams baseball cards that maybe you want to throw away?"

Sammy shook his head and grinned. He then pointed to a chair occupying a corner next to his counter. "All right, Brian. Go and sit in that corner for one hour," came the unexpected teasing.

But, Brian wasn't through with his act. He looked at the astonished young faces who witnessed his performance and said, "It's okay, they let me out of the institution for two hours every day. They'll be here soon to pick me up."

Sammy didn't know whether to get mad or to laugh out loud. He watched as Brian lumbered over to the chair, sat, and displayed a big mechanical grin on his face. One young, potential customer, not knowing what to believe, slowly backed up, spun around, and hurried to his mother's side.

"Look who just came in," said Brian, nudging his partner's arm.

Sammy scanned the customers and noted the newcomer. "Hi, Mr. Stoltzfus. How's the lawn furniture business?"

Mrs. Wilson stuck her head out of the quilt room, "Hello, Amos. You here to see my husband?"

"Yes, when he ain't busy," said Amos, who didn't miss the fact that Mr. Wilson was in the middle of a credit card transaction.

Without looking up, Mr. Wilson said, "Be with you in a minute, Amos."

Amos saw the newspaper lying on the register counter where Brian had flipped it earlier. "You mind if I take a look over your paper? I want to read myself full of news."

"No, go ahead," said Mr. Wilson.

"I just want to check to see who stopped drinking coffee and who started to drink milk," commented Amos as he skimmed through the paper.

Brian was puzzled. He glanced at Sammy and whispered, "What's he mean by that?"

"Oh, he wants to see who died and who was born."

It took a while for Brian to sift through that one. "Makes sense."

"I think it's an Amish expression," added Sammy.

"Hey, anybody here named Sammy Wilson?" voiced a tourist, waving an envelope in his hand.

"Yeah, here," said Sammy, coming out from behind the counter.

"This envelope has your name on it," said the tourist. "Found it taped to your front door there."

"Huh, thanks." Sammy was mystified. He opened the envelope and returned behind the counter. The note was short and to the point. After Sammy read it, he was stunned. He leaned to his right and showed it to Brian. It read: STAY OUT OF SOMETHING THAT DOES NOT CONCERN YOU - OR YOU DIE TOO!

Chapter Ten

The note's message was clear. Forget about the dead body: Victor Marsh. Forget about the burglary or die. Brian glanced up at Sammy and swallowed hard. "Someone wants us to back off."

"That's a good sign," said Sammy. "We're getting close."

"Yeah, close to death." Brian stood up. "I'd rather not become fuel for someone's fire."

Sammy turned his attention to three boys who wanted various packs of cards and a rookie card from inside the glass case. He then directed them to the "man at the cash register" to pay for them. One child, who consulted his own father, had to return two out of the four packs because the cost was beyond his allowance.

Without warning, a huge figure emerged through the front door. His size and presence demanded your attention, especially in a small merchandise-filled room. Several tourists moved to one of the other three smaller rooms. Sammy and Brian beamed hopeful smiles of recognition to Detective Ben Phillips.

"Hello," said the detective as he passed Mr. Wilson on his way back to see the boys. He projected a hugh grin as he slid behind the counter, which didn't leave much room for the three of them. However, it provided the secrecy that was needed for the forthcoming confidential information.

"Sammy, your hunch was right." Phillips held up one of the photos Sammy had given him the day before. "Warden Packard of the New York State Prison identified this man as Harry Belmont. And what do you know? This Belmont was Victor Marsh's cell mate until he was released two years ago."

Sammy felt good, like getting an A+ for a perfect paper. It was pay- back time for putting the pieces together in the correct order. Now he had everything he needed. Everything that is except evidence. He still needed some answers from yesterday's truck experience. The teenagers also decided not to tell Detective Phillips about the ordeal. He looked at Phillips, pressed his lips together, and raised his eyebrows. "Now all we need is proof. We have to prove that Harry Belmont killed Victor Marsh."

"Not only that," said Brian, "but, but . . . show him the note, Sammy."

Phillips read the threatening note. "Harry Belmont knows you're onto him. Is that the way it goes down?"

Sammy's blue eyes were downcast. "Yep," he said.

"Oh, and one more bit of information," said Phillips. "Victor Marsh *was* murdered. Shot with a .25-caliber gun. And not at the tobacco shed. The medical examiner's report says he was killed somewhere else and then transported to the shed."

"I'll bet with the same gun pointed at our backs the other night when we were lying on the floor," said Brian. He sat back down on his chair. "I wonder why he didn't shoot us?"

"He didn't have to," explained the detective. "He wasn't under the amount of pressure with you boys as he was with Victor. Victor knew him and what kind of scum he was. But you boys weren't a threat because you couldn't prove anything. He was wearing the bird suit and didn't talk."

Sammy was trying to put all the available pieces together. "We have to prove that Harry Belmont shot him and then dumped him into the shed and set it on fire."

"It could take a long time," offered Phillips, "before we can collect enough evidence. And we *can* collect evidence. You see, whenever a crime is committed something is always either brought to the crime scene or taken from the crime scene."

"Exactly what do you mean by that?" asked Brian.

"Well, we know Victor Marsh was shot and killed somewhere other than Beiler's tobacco shed. Blood, hair, bullet holes in a wall or such could have been left behind where he was killed. If the body was transported in a car, there could be evidence of blood, hairs, or particles of clothing found in the trunk. Now at Andy Beiler's shed . . ."

"That's the last piece of the puzzle!" yelled Sammy. "Yes, that's it!"

He didn't intend to create a stir in the shop, but heads did turn his way. Eyes scrutinized the large, ominous bulk that overshadowed the two helpless teenagers. Was the man doing bodily harm to the young boys?

"Oh, I'm sorry," said Sammy to anyone who might be listening. "Everything's all right." He quickly returned to the previous conversation. "I had the piece of the puzzle to solve this case but didn't recognize it. And with your permission and help, Detective Phillips, here's what we need to do . . ."

Chapter Eleven

Several out-of-state charter buses had arrived, spilling the tourists out onto the Farmer's Market asphalt parking lot. After the new arrivals organized themselves into friendly groups, some charged toward the market. Others were fascinated by a passing horse and buggy and hurried to Main Street. Still others headed straight for the old village stores that were scattered along Main Street, otherwise known as the Old Philadelphia Pike or Route 340. But the most observant of the tourists saw the colorful, animated bird, elevated on a painted plywood hand in the corner of the parking lot.

According to a large sign attached to the plywood hand, Saturday, today, at one o'clock, The Bird would be unmasked. The sign also thanked everyone who had donated to the David Lapp Barn Raising Fund. The identity of The Bird and the amount of money collected would be revealed at one o'clock.

Many of the curious tourists who did venture over to the platform asked questions of the local citizens. Even though the fund-raiser had officially ended the day before, volunteers were still behind tables accepting donations and answering the tourists' questions about Amish barn raisings.

Visitors were told the Amish barn raising is a social event. Hundreds of Amish friends and relatives gather to donate their time and skills to raise a barn and put it under roof in one day. The Amish men do the actual carpentry work while the Amish women cook and serve the meals. If the cost of the new barn cannot be met by the farmer, money is available from a special insurance fund set up by the farmers. The David Lapp Fund was to be yet another source of financial help, thanks to the generosity of the Bird-In-Hand community.

Inside the Farmer's Market, the two teenage detectives positioned themselves as planned at Brenda's snack bar. Waiting and eating. Earlier, with the help of his father, Sammy had gone back to the Amish farm to retrieve the bikes. While there, he had an informative talk with Jacob Esh who owned the farm. All of the young detective's questions had been answered at that time. The remaining puzzle pieces could now be slipped into place.

"Boys, The Bird has me stymied," said Brenda from behind the counter. "I've talked to people, and I've asked myself, who in Bird-In-Hand would be willing to suffocate in a bird costume for five and a half days? I really couldn't come up with a name. So I did some detective work and took a guess anyway."

"Whose name did you enter?" asked Brian.

"Mary Witmer. Do you know her?"

Sammy glanced at Brian. "Brian knows her real well. *Right, Brian?*"

The expression on Brian's face didn't change. He was waiting for Brenda to explain her decision.

"She works over at the bake shop," continued Brenda. "Hasn't been there all this week."

"Sounds like a good choice to me," said Brian as he lowered his head and smiled. What he had not told Sammy was that the day before, he had made another donation and entered another name in the contest. He wasn't positively sure, but this time he might have a chance at topping his good friend. Wouldn't it be great, he thought, if just this once he could come in first. After all, miracles do happen, and he had made himself a promise.

"Well, Brian, it's almost one o'clock," announced Sammy. "Time to go."

Two wrinkled napkins, two small empty paper plates, and two used plastic forks remained on the counter as the boys swiveled off the stools and headed for the unmasking.

Since Saturday was a busy tourist day, a crowd engulfed the Bird in the Hand platform. The tourists were there to experience the local charm and color; the locals were there to find out the amount of money collected and the identity of The Bird. Detective Ben Phillips, Sammy Wilson, Brian Helm, several plainclothes policemen, and a police woman wanted to make an arrest with the least amount of commotion possible.

Sammy and Brian worked their way to the front of the platform to claim a spot. From their vantage point they could see Chet Kelley, dressed in shorts and a sport shirt, looking much like a tourist, standing to the left of the stage. To the right, Norman Snyder and Buddy Kline were together, leaning against a truck. Near the stage, Amos Stoltzfus was waiting to receive the money that had been donated to the David Lapp Fund. David Lapp, his wife and children, and several other Amish friends from his church district were on hand to acknowledge their appreciation for the donations.

"Well, the time has come," yelled Gil Green from the platform, "to reveal the person who prevailed five days and this morning in the bird disguise. Who is The Bird? I would like to announce we have one winner. Yes, one of our own townsfolk correctly guessed the person in the costume and will win the prizes. But before we tell you about that, I'm going to have The Bird step forward and display cards. The cards will show the names and donations of local companies, plus the total amount of money donated to the David Lapp Fund. "Okay, Bird, take over." Gil Green turned and left the stage.

As The Bird displayed the cards one at a time, the boys slowly edged their way around the platform and headed for a white Camaro parked behind it.

Harry Belmont had just slammed the door shut and was turning the key in the ignition. The engine wouldn't start. He tried again and heard only a grinding noise.

"Having car trouble?" asked Detective Phillips, walking up to the open car window.

An unmarked police car pulled in front of the white Camaro while another police car was already parked behind. Sammy and Brian joined the encounter as a plainclothes policewoman suddenly appeared on the opposite side of the Camaro.

"Were you going somewhere, Gil Green, or should I call you Harry Belmont?" Detective Phillips' heavy voice and weighty frame compounded the question. "According to the Lancaster Airport, a Mr. Harry Belmont has a one-way ticket to Chicago on the two-thirty flight."

Green glanced around and was surprised to see his car surrounded. "What's going on here? Who are you?"

The detective whipped out a paper with his left hand and unsnapped a wallet and exposed a police shield with his right. "I'm Detective Ben Phillips of the police department, and I have a search warrant to seize and search your car. Please take off your shoes and step out of the car." The detective opened the car door.

Harry Belmont swiveled to the left, took off his shoes, and grudgingly shoved them at the detective.

"Put your hands on your head where I can see them." Phillips kept his eyes on Belmont and passed the shoes over to a plainclothes policeman.

"There's something wrong here. You have the wrong man. I'm Gilbert Green, businessman," said Harry Belmont as he awkwardly maneuvered out of the Camaro and stood up, keeping his hands on his head.

One of the plainclothes policemen stepped forward and patted him down. He was clean, no weapons.

"I have a document here that says you're Harry Belmont, con man," replied Phillips. "It's a report from a friend of yours, Warden Packard of the New York State Prison. The report contains a picture and fingerprints of a Harry Belmont, who until a few years ago, shared a prison cell with Victor Marsh."

Sammy took over. "When Victor Marsh hollered out, 'Hey, I know who you are,' he was referring to you, *not* The Bird. When he recognized you, he realized at once you were pulling another scam. Now where was Mr. Marsh going to get all that cash he was bragging about? By blackmailing you, Mr. Belmont."

Belmont was trapped, but he wouldn't give up. "But, I didn't know the man in the crowd was Victor Marsh."

Sammy pressed onward. "On Tuesday, the day after Mr. Marsh showed up, I talked to you outside our shop. You said something to me that proved you *had known* Mr. Marsh before. You mentioned something about the tattooed snakes on his wrists. There's no way you could have identified those tattoos from where you were standing on the platform. Mr. Marsh was standing near Brian and me in the rear of the crowd. You remembered the tattoos either from your jail time with him, or you saw them when you met Mr. Marsh later on Monday."

"Now, how could you know that?"

"Do you still have the business card from our store?"

"Yes, but . . ."

Phillips extended the palm of his hand. "I'd like to see that card, please."

"Yes, here." He slowly lowered his right hand and slid his wallet from his pants pocket. He found the card and handed it to the detective.

Phillips noted the telephone number on the back. "So Victor Marsh confronted you on Monday. He demanded money or he would blow the whole, sweet operation you had going here. Marsh was desperate for money. He owed big bucks to a loan shark in New York. I found this out from Chet Kelley, an enforcer, who followed Marsh here. Kelley was instructed to collect the money or break bones. So you were going to be Victor's way out. Victor wrote the telephone number where he could be reached on the back of this card and gave it to you."

"That simply is not true. You can't prove that. The telephone number is for a motel. One of my investors was staying there."

"Well then," added Sammy, "how do you explain the other writing that's also here on the back? It's the name and the price of a quilt that *I* wrote on this card and gave to Mr. Marsh when he visited our shop Monday."

Harry Belmont was dumbfounded. "All right, Vic confronted me Monday night. He demanded money.

Said he wanted it the next day. He wrote his phone number on the card and insisted I call him. When I called the next day, I told him to do whatever he wanted; I wouldn't pay blackmail. I never saw Vic after that."

"Take a look at what I found," came a voice from the back of the car, "a .25-caliber revolver and a suitcase full of money."

All heads turned to the rear of the car. All heads except one. Harry Belmont reached over, grabbed Brian, and quickly pressured a ballpoint pen against the teenager's neck. "Everybody back or I kill the boy!"

Belmont backed up, dragging the young detective in front of him.

Brian was white. Much later he would think of all the tricks he could have used to escape. But, not now. Now, he could only feel the deadly writing instrument pressed against his neck.

No one moved. The man was desperate, an ex-con who had killed and would kill again rather than go back to jail. They waited to see what Belmont would do next.

At a safer distance away from the police, Belmont lessened the pressure of the ballpoint pen, allowing Brian to move faster. After all, he didn't want to accidentally stab the boy. He needed Brian alive as a hostage until he made good his escape. He quickly glanced back to be sure he was headed for the Bird in the Hand platform and Norman Snyder's truck parked nearby.

It was difficult for Sammy to watch Brian being hauled off by the hardened killer. Here he was, an intelligent problem solver of puzzles and mysteries who had outsmarted criminals before. This time he didn't know how to save his friend from the hands of a murderer. Once before on another case, he thought he had lost his best friend. Now he felt guilty for getting Brian into this mess. Then he saw hope. Glancing at Phillips, who saw the same promise, he said "Let's do it."

Both of them ran toward Harry Belmont followed by the backup team.

"Hey, stay back!" shouted Belmont. "Do you think I'm kidding?" He pulled Brian closer and raised the pen for them to see. "This is a real sharp pen here."

With all the color and action of a television show, a red, yellow, and blue pile of feathers landed on the head and shoulders of the con man. Two feathered wings grabbed his face and invaded his mouth, nose, and eyes. Surprised and in a state of bewilderment, Belmont loosened his grip, allowing Brian to pull free and the pen to fall to the ground. The Bird had made a grand, flying leap from the stage and now continued to have a one-sided pillow fight with real feathers.

Norman Snyder and Buddy Kline were the first to reach and seize the struggling murderer.

"Get this animal off of me." Belmont clutched at the mass of activity on his head only to end up with blobs of feathers in his hands.

With Norman and Buddy hanging on, Phillips cuffed one hand then swung around Belmont, captured the other hand, and forced it around to join the other in handcuffs. Looking at the two men and breathing hard, Phillips said, "Thanks for the assist."

Up to this point the crowd had been passive. All of the donations made by local businesses had been displayed. The total money collected, $34,782, had been posted. Everyone was waiting for Gil Green to return to unmask The Bird. They had not been aware of the police encounter that took place behind the platform. But, when they saw The Bird in flight, and the apparent antics between it and Gil Green, cheers and applause exploded in the parking lot.

Ben Phillips untangled the feathered superhero from Belmont's face and gently helped The Bird to a chair next to the platform. After he was sure The Bird and Brian were okay, he instructed his officers to take Harry Belmont and the Camaro to the station.

Amos Stoltzfus had seen Gil Green's confrontation with the police and knew it was now up to him to bring David Lapp's fund-raiser to a close. He didn't bother with the stage. He stood by The Bird and announced, "We had a little excitement here oncest, a little police matter. But, everything's all right now. So let's just put The Bird out of its misery." Amos carefully lifted the head mask and was immediately befuddled. He studied the face but did not recognize it. "Does anyone know who it is?"

Chapter Twelve

The hair was plastered to the head, perspiration and redness covered the thin face. A frail voice crept from the mouth. "Hi, it's me."

"That's my mother," said Brian. His face, which had regained some of its color, sported a wide grin.

"Yeah, what's left of me. I must have lost twenty pounds."

"Sorry, but you puzzled me so," said Amos, who now recognized Mrs. Helm. He turned and faced the onlookers. "The Bird is Sue Helm, Brian Helm's mother."

A wave of applause swept in toward Sue Helm. She rose from the chair and acknowledged their tribute by waving two battle-worn wings. Some loose feathers floated and swirled to the ground.

"Okay, there are a lot more exciting things to see here in Bird-In-Hand," announced Detective

Phillips, aiming the statement at the tourists. "The party's over here."

Sammy was stunned when Brian was immediately able to identify The Bird as his mother, when he had trouble himself recognizing her. He watched as Brian and his mother hugged each other. "Brian, why do I get the impression that you knew your mother was The Bird?"

"Oh, you didn't know?" Brian was going to rub it in, now that he felt somewhat relieved having escaped injury or death, thanks to his mother. "I did just what you told me to do. Through clever detective work, I collected three clues to add to your three clues."

"That's great!" said Sammy. "What were your three clues?"

"You remember when we were sweating in the truck? You mentioned it made you think of the person being hot and losing weight in the bird suit. That statement made me think about my mother wanting to lose weight. She would also be away for the exact length of time The Bird existed.

"And what was your third fact?" asked Sammy.

"We saw a light on at my house the other night. When those three facts are put together with your three facts, any detective worth his salt would come to the same conclusion: Mrs. Helm did not leave town, but was in fact living at home at night and was wearing the bird costume during the day. It's just elementary, my dear Sammy."

"Brian, you are developing into a fine detective," said Detective Phillips. "And you boys have a job at the station anytime you want it."

"Hey, I just remembered," said Brian, "I won a one-hundred-dollar saving bond and four tickets to Hersheypark."

"I'm sorry to tell you this, dear," said Mrs. Helm as she and the feathered costume squeezed her son and kissed the top of his head, "but members of the family are not eligible for the prize."

The disappointment lasted for a few seconds. Brian then stood wobbly but tall and said, "That's okay, Sammy and I don't take rewards for our detective work. Right, Sammy?"

"You are right, Brian. You are exactly right." Sammy was glad to have his best friend back, unharmed and his old self again. He stooped and retrieved some feathers from the asphalt. "Brian, greatness must run in your family. Your mother showed courage and bravery when she jumped on Mr. Belmont like that."

"Oh, no, not really," said Mrs. Helm, putting her winged arm around Brian again. "You see, I had to; my son was in danger. She looked confused as she asked, "Wasn't that Gil Green I landed on?"

Detective Phillips answered. "His real name is Harry Belmont and the whole fund-raiser was a scam along with his Amish Virtual Reality scheme. He fooled everyone into believing he was doing them a favor. He has the appearance of a person you can trust. A real con man. And he would have gotten away with murder and all the money, too, if it hadn't been for Sammy and Brian."

"How did you catch onto him, Sammy?" asked Mrs. Helm.

"It was really Brian who developed the first clue."

"Yeah, I said, 'Who are you saying good luck to, The Bird or Mr. Green?'" added Brian, who didn't mind at all that his mother was still hugging him.

Sammy leaned against the base of the stage. "That got me thinking about the tattooed man, Victor Marsh, when he yelled, 'I know who you are.' He wasn't talking about The Bird; he was talking about his old prison buddy, Harry Belmont, alias, Gil Green. And since Marsh ended up dead after saying he was going to get his hands on a lot of money, it all pointed to Harry Belmont. Thanks to you, Mrs. Helm, Brian and I were able to collect enough clues to support a probable cause warrant."

Sue Helm appeared surprised. "Me? How did I do that?"

"According to Mr. Belmont, you were changing in and out of costume in the bathroom of the storefront business he was renting."

"Yes, I did, but, how . . .?"

"One evening when you left, I believe you forgot to lock the back door, and that allowed Brian and me to enter and find the carton boxes."

"Yes, it's possible I forgot to lock the door," said Sue. "I was so glad and in a hurry to get out of that suit and get home." She pictured the piles of boxes. "Was something wrong with the cartons?"

"They were all empty," answered Sammy. "Mr. Belmont displayed the elaborately labeled boxes to impress his would-be investors on the size and quality of the electronic equipment. The way Brian and I have it figured, Mr. Belmont saw us when we entered the unlocked back door to his office that night. He realized it wouldn't take us long to discover that the cartons were empty. So he devised a plan, fake a burglary. He snuck in through the back door, put on the bird costume so we wouldn't recognize him, and then overpowered us with his gun. He then taped our hands and feet and our eyes so we couldn't interfere with or see him go through the motions of a burglary."

Amos Stoltzfus asked, "But how did you know all the boxes were empty oncest?"

"When Brian accidentally knocked a pile over, we realized they were empty but taped shut. Later when I brushed against another stack while hiding, they felt light and moved easily. It was several days later I realized the tape Amos removed from us, was the same kind of tape used to seal the empty cartons. All the carton boxes that were cut open during the pretend robbery had been sealed with the same kind of tape. Mr. Belmont apparently had gotten his hands on empty boxes a company had discarded and taped them shut so they would appear full and unopened."

Brian straightened up and combed his fingers through his curly brown hair. "Mr. Belmont couldn't pull the tape over our eyes. Right, Sammy?"

Sammy was glad his best friend was back to normal. "Speaking of tape, when The Bird was taping me and had his foot on my shoulder, I detected a strong odor. I couldn't place it until later when Detective Phillips mentioned evidence could be taken away from a crime scene. Then it registered. The smell was tobacco dust, ground into the murderer's shoes from Andy Beiler's tobacco shed."

"These were the same shoes I took from Belmont at his car. From the smell of them," said Phillips, "the lab will have no trouble getting a sample of dust to analyze."

"There is something though, about that night, that I don't understand," admitted Sammy. "Mr. Stoltzfus, why were you at Harry Belmont's office?"

"To tell you boys the truth," said Amos, "I thought something mighty smelly was going on. Gil Green, or what's his new name now, Harry? He wouldn't give me the donation money. He wasn't even putting the money in the bank. Every day he said he would, but he don't. He didn't look good in the face. That night I just came by and saw the light and invited myself in to figure him out some. Lucky for you boys yet, huh."

"Lucky for everybody except Harry Belmont," said Detective Phillips. "When the lab checks his gun and analyzes every hair, stain, and dirt particle found in his car, we'll have him for murder and arson."

"It's hard to believe," said Sammy, "that he would torch an Amish barn so he could create a fund-raiser and steal the money."

"Belmont was running two scams at one time," added Phillips. "From the looks of his operation, he conned the local investors out of over a hundred thousand dollars."

"Didn't I tell you, boys," said Norman, "that someone was going to get killed.? Yes. I told you. It's terrible, terrible. Crime in our little, peaceful village."

Sammy moved closer to Norman. "But, we caught the bad guy. You helped us, and you can be proud of that. Something else you can be proud of, Mr. Snyder. I understand you helped Mr. Kline get part-time work."

"Yes," answered Buddy Kline. "He introduced me to Jacob Esh who was looking for an 'English' person with a car to provide transportation when he needs it."

"So that's what they were doing at the Amish farm," said Brian. "But, who locked us in the truck?"

Sammy shrugged his shoulders. "I can make a guess. Two cars followed us from the police station. Mr. Kelley in the blue Ford and Mr. Belmont in another. Both men were interested in what the police and we had learned about Mr. Marsh. After our encounter with Mr. Kelley, Mr. Belmont followed us as we rode our bikes behind the truck to the Amish farm. He locked us in the truck to scare us and then followed through with the warning note at the shop."

"I don't know about you people, but I'm tired, and I must get back to the station," said Phillips. "Oh, by the way, Amos, you'll have to wait until after the trial before we can return David Lapp's fund money to you."

"Ach, we Amish had the barn raising long already," said Amos, "but the bills can wait." He tipped his yellow straw hat back on his forehead and said, "When things need done, we do. When things need wait, we do that too yet."

Everyone smiled and shook their heads in agreement.

Sue Helm nudged her son. "Come on, Brian, let's go home where it's safe, and I can have a life outside of this bird suit."

"Sammy, you know what I think?" asked Brian as he locked in on his dramatic posture. "I just got to thinking, it can be dangerous being your friend. I don't want to be your buddy anymore. My mommy bird and I are going home now. I don't want to see you anymore, Sammy. Our friendship is over. I am leaving you forever, forever."

Sammy smiled. "Okay, if that's the way you feel about it. See you Monday."

Brian and his mother walked away.

"Yep, see you Monday," said Brian.

SAMMY AND BRIAN MYSTERIES

☐ The Quilted Message

by Ken Munro

The whole village was talking about it. Did the Amish quilt contain more than just twenty mysterious cloth pictures? The pressure was on for Bird-In-Hand's two teenage detectives, Sammy and Brian, to solve the mystery. Was Amos King murdered because of the quilt? Who broke into the country store? It was time for Sammy and Brian to unmask the intruder. $4.95

☐ Bird in the Hand

by Ken Munro

When arson is suspected on an Amish farm, the village of Bird-In-Hand responds with a fund-raiser. The appearance of a mysterious tattooed man starts a series of events that ends in murder. And who is The Bird? Only Bird-In-Hand's own teenage detectives can unravel the mystery. ~~$4.95~~ $5.95

Buy them at your local bookstore or use this convenient coupon for ordering.

Gaslight Publishers
P.O. Box 258
Bird-In-Hand, PA 17505

Please send me the books I have checked above.

I am enclosing $____(please add $2.00 for postage and handling). Send check or money order only.

Name ____
Address ______________________________________
City ________________ State ______ Zip Code _________